TODD CAMPBELL

The Everyday Adventurer Series - Move Like a Rogue

Contents

About the Series

The Everyday Adventurer is a series of motivational books inspired by the legendary fantasy classes found in tabletop role-playing games.

Each volume focuses on a different archetype. Not as escapism, but as a lens for real-life transformation. Classes offer us a language for understanding ourselves. They shape how we make decisions under pressure, how we handle conflict, and how we choose our next move when things stop working. They help us see ourselves not as stuck or broken but as players still learning the skills of our path. They remind us we can adapt, choose differently, and grow, always. Whether you're drawn to the precision of the Rogue, the intelligence of the Wizard, the courage of the Paladin, or even the discipline of the Monk, each archetype reflects a part of who you are and who you could become.

These aren't books about gaming. They're about playing life differently.

Each chapter blends real stories, actionable strategies, science, and reflection to help you "level up" in your world.

This book walks with the Rogue.

The observer.
The strategist.
The quiet disruptor.

The one who understands that timing, subtlety, and awareness change everything.

Each class stands alone, yet connects to the others. Each book is a path you can walk in any order. Wherever you begin is the right place.

Your class is just the beginning.

Your adventure is already underway.

How to Use This Book

This isn't a book you read once and shelve. It's a toolkit.

You won't find everything in one pass. You're not supposed to. Rogues don't carry everything. They carry what's useful. This book works the same way. Take what hits, leave the rest, and come back when the moment calls for it.

You're not here to be perfect. You're here to move smarter.

This book isn't meant to be finished for the sake of finishing, and it isn't here to turn you into a literal Rogue. There are no tricks, cheat codes, or hidden exploits waiting in these pages. What you'll find instead are ways of thinking, noticing, and choosing that you can apply in real moments, between meetings, conversations, and decisions that actually matter. Progress here doesn't come from reading straight through. It comes from using one idea at the right time, then coming back when the next move calls for it.

This book is meant to be:

- Read in silence or in short bursts. Whatever suits your rhythm
- Used as a personal guide, not a rigid playbook
- Revisited when your path shifts, or when you do

Each chapter includes:

- A story or insight to reframe how you think
- A mindset or move drawn from the Rogue's path
- A small, real-world tactic or challenge to help you act with intention
- A named action move that matches the role you are training in that section

Some chapters will land like a critical hit, while others might not speak to you yet. That's fine. You're not here to collect every move, you're here to use what works.

Pro Tip: Start a notes doc, journal, or Notion page. Track the tools that resonate, the habits you've tested, the exits you've mapped, the roles you've dropped, and the doors you've left unopened. This is your Rogue Kit. Let it grow with your experience.

Reading Paths

New to the path? Start at the beginning and walk it all the way through. **Facing something specific?** Flip to the chapter that fits your moment. **Need a quick dose of clarity?** Let the book ambush you. Open to a random page and trust what you find.

You don't have to unlock every door to get value. You just have to pick the first lock.

A Note on the Code

Throughout this book, you'll see terms like stealth, trap, escape plan, and skill check.

These aren't game mechanics.

They're real-world metaphors, drawn from the Rogue's way of moving through life.

You don't need to play RPGs to understand them. If anything ever feels unclear, flip to The Rogue's Pocket Guide in the back for a quick breakdown of the most-used terms. It's there to help, not test you.

This isn't about pretending to be a Rogue. It's about thinking like one and moving like one too.

Let's begin. Not with a map, but with a moment. A move. A question that won't wait.

You Don't Need Permission to Move

The Rogue's Path Begins

I've always loved characters who worked in the background. The ones who didn't need a spotlight to change the outcome. The ones who paid attention while everyone else was performing. I never thought I was one growing up, but the more I lived, the more I began to understand how powerful that kind of presence really is.

Not everyone is loud.
Not everyone fights with force.

Some people move quietly. They read the room and wait for the right moment. That kind of move doesn't happen by accident. It's built in silence, observation, and restraint. Most people miss the Rogue's work because it happens before anything goes wrong.

Rogues don't win because they're the strongest or fastest. They win because they see what others miss. They prepare, they pivot, and they move with intention.

There may be no treasure chests or trapdoors in real life, but there are pressure plates, hidden doors, and decisions that ask for more than brute strength. You don't have to fight your way forward. Sometimes the smartest move is knowing when to listen, when to leave, and when to slip through the side door before anyone else sees it.

Here's what this book means when it says *Rogue*:

The Rogue isn't a thief or a trickster. The Rogue is anyone who learns to move through life on their own terms. They don't wait for permission. They study patterns, find openings, and act when others freeze. Being a Rogue means learning to navigate systems, relationships, and obstacles. It's about freedom through strategy, not rebellion for its own sake.

When this book talks about the shadows, it isn't about hiding or darkness. It's the background. The quiet space where thought and instinct meet. Where you're watching, learning, and deciding before anyone realizes a move is being made.

You don't have to be sneaky to be strategic. You don't have to be silent to be smart. You just have to start paying attention.

First, the world. Then, yourself. That's how awareness sharpens.

The Rogue's Path

You don't need a dagger or a disguise.

To be a Rogue in this life, all you need is a sharpened instinct and the courage to move your own way. This book is your toolkit. A space to observe, reflect, and move through the world with clarity and precision.

The shifts are subtle. The habits are sharp. The impact is quiet. The effect is unmistakable. This isn't a spotlight path. It's a strategy path.

Welcome to the Rogue's path.

I

The Cutpurse

Rogues don't start at the center. They begin at the edges. They watch, they wait, and they learn the rules before choosing which ones to break. Life in the margins sharpens your eyes. You adapt to stay unseen and survive by learning fast. This part is about turning quiet strengths into sharp strategy. You can't master the situation until you learn to watch it.

The world watches the loud ones.
The Rogue watches the world.
This is where your edge begins.

The Rogue's Path

Every shift begins unnoticed. A glance at the clock, a sigh over coffee, or a thought that won't leave like, *This isn't working*.

No fanfare.
No cue.

Just a quiet pull toward something else. Most people wait for a sign, an invitation, the moment that proves they're ready. They want someone to look them in the eye and say, *"Now's the time. You're allowed. You're chosen."* Until then, they wait. Sometimes for years.

Rogues don't wait.

Not because they're fearless, but because they've stopped expecting permission. The Rogue's journey doesn't begin with celebration. It starts when you realize no one's coming to save you, and weirdly, that realization doesn't break you. It sharpens you.

You get quiet.
You get clear.

You move.

You won't feel ready. That's part of the story, and that's the trick of it. Rogues move while still shaking. They act before the story is sure it wants to begin. Readiness isn't a condition for starting. It's the reward that comes after, but no one tells you that. You think the nerves mean you're not meant for this. You think that fear is a stop sign.

The Rogue knows better. They recognize that feeling as a compass. Fear that points toward growth, not away from it. If you're scared but still leaning in, you're probably on the right path.

That's the path. It doesn't begin with mastery. It begins with instinct, movement, and figuring things out as you go.

The Cutpurse Mentality

The Cutpurse doesn't start as a master thief or a master anything. They start unknowing, seeing, listening, learning. Their beginning is rough, but honest. That's where most of us begin. Figuring things out by trying, missing, failing, and then adjusting on the fly.

No special training.
No secret backing.
Just instinct and drive.

It's not about finesse yet, it's about getting by. Watching, adapting, then taking your shot, even if your hand shakes when you reach. It's the kind of energy that knows how to move through a room without being noticed. That knows how to stretch a dollar, fix something with tape and hope, and read five people at once just to stay ahead. You don't get that from books.

You get it from needing to figure it out before something breaks. The

Cutpurse isn't concerned with prestige, they're just trying to keep going. They learn fast because they have to. They build skills in silence. They steal time back from bad situations, and then they turn it into leverage. No one claps for them, but later, people wonder how they got so sharp. You may not feel like a Rogue. You might not even be sure what you're doing yet. If you've ever moved on your own, without approval, without applause, you're already walking this path.

The Cutpurse doesn't wait for mastery. They move with what they've got. I know that feeling well. I've lived it.

When I Made My Move

A few years back, I left my job to start my own business. I did what people say you're supposed to do. I saved money, found the idea, and then bought a business that had been around for over twenty years. It was a mobile disc and drum mechanic service. I drove from shop to shop, machining brake rotors and drums out of the back of a van. There was no storefront, no team, just me, the tools, and the road.

At first, it worked. The old clients were calling, money was coming in, and I thought, *This is it. I did it. This was the right move.*

One morning, I headed out with quiet confidence in my chest. It said *maybe, just maybe, things were going to work out.* I could see it. A steady income, a growing route, something I could be proud of. I started imagining what life might look like a year down the road. I imagined my life with no money worries, weekends off, and the ability to start going on vacations with the family. I even started thinking of the van as mine, not just physically, but spiritually. That van was more than a vehicle. It was the heart of the business, and I wanted to build something people remembered.

Then the calls slowed down, and then they just stopped.

I tried new angles. Called old contacts. Lowered my prices. I even offered add-ons for free.

Nothing.

I learned my services weren't in demand the way they used to be. Shops could now buy brand new rotors for less than it cost to have me machine them. It wasn't personal, it was just brutal market math. In three months, I had to sell everything just to get a little money back.

No sugarcoating it. It felt like a failure, and I felt like a failure. I had put everything into that move. Time, savings, belief, and when it crumbled, it didn't just hurt my plans. It bruised my identity. I wasn't just losing a business. I was losing the story I had started to tell myself. That I could finally be the one who made it. Maybe this time, I'd pulled it off. I remember packing up the van, piece by piece, staring at the tools that just weeks before had felt like the keys to my future. Now they were just weight. Even the sound of metal hitting the van bed felt different, like the clink of coins you lost in a bet you were sure you'd win, but I kept going.

I took what I learned and used it, one choice at a time. It shaped my path, my work, my life. Now? This is where I've landed. Writing these books is my next adventure. That moment didn't break me. It changed me. You don't need to win to keep moving. What you learn from falling often lasts longer than any win. Sometimes, falling on your face teaches you how to move quieter, smarter, and closer to the ground.

Alone doesn't mean lost. Sometimes, it's the only place a real beginning can happen.

No Party, No Problem

People love the idea of building something with a team. A support system, a circle of believers, and that's nice when it happens, but it's not always how things start. Sometimes, you're it. The first and only believer in your idea. The only one willing to risk the move. That's how the Cutpurse begins.

Alone.
Unproven.
Uninvited.

That's not a weakness. It's part of the training, and there were nights where I doubted everything. Where I second-guessed the entire path. Where I'd stare at a screen, wondering if I'd just wasted months of effort on a dead idea, and no one texted to say "keep going." There was no applause, no safety net, but I kept moving, and eventually, someone noticed. Someone saw the spark and said, "Hey, this is something." That moment hit harder than any crowd ever could, because I knew it wasn't built on hype.

It was real.

When you have to carry your own vision, your own doubts, and your own direction, it makes you sharper, more focused, more tuned into what matters, and when people do come along later, you'll know how to choose wisely. You'll remember who showed up after you had already started walking.

The Cutpurse doesn't wait to be picked. They move first and let the right people catch up.

Motion Over Permission

We're trained to think we need permission from bosses, mentors, institutions, even friends. The Rogue learns early that waiting doesn't get you anywhere. Before I embraced this mindset, I used to over-ask. I'd wait for someone to say it was okay, that I was qualified, that it was time. I would mistake politeness for planning or caution for wisdom.

Now? I move first.

The Cutpurse doesn't ask to join the game. They slide into it quietly, undetected. They don't wait for a gate to open. They find the gap in the fence. The best part? Once you stop waiting for permission, you see doors where everyone else sees walls, because Rogue movement isn't about reckless leaps. It's about seeing the cracks, the timing, the rhythm of the room. There was a season in my life where I asked for a green light from everyone. Before every move, I'd float the idea. I would ask for feedback, wait for the consensus, but deep down, I wasn't looking for advice. I was looking for permission, and when it didn't come, I stalled.

Looking back, those were some of the most frustrating chapters of my life. Not because I didn't have ideas, but because I didn't trust myself enough to act on them alone. The Rogue in me hadn't woken up yet, but it was there, and once I realized I was the only one who could choose my direction, everything shifted. You may not know everything, you may not feel ready, but movement sharpens you in ways waiting never will. Even if it's a small step, even if it doesn't work out.

You become your own map.

From Edges to Advantage

When you live on the edges, you develop a different kind of awareness. You learn to read tone, to pick up subtle shifts, to know when to speak and when to vanish. It's not about being paranoid. It's about pattern recognition. You're not loud, but you're observant. You don't demand attention, but you pay attention. That changes how you move through rooms, conversations, decisions. You've probably been there. In the meeting no one thought you had a stake in, maybe the social setting where you didn't "belong", or the job you had to figure out on your own.

You watched.
You learned.
You moved.

That's not just survival. That's skill. From the outside looking in, it may not seem powerful, but being underestimated is one of the Rogue's greatest tools.

The world can't block what it doesn't see coming.

The Rogue's First Step

This is the truth. If you've read this far, you've already stepped onto the path.

Maybe you're unsure. Maybe it's slow. Maybe you don't even have a name for what you're building.

That's okay. That's how most actual paths begin. Rogues don't wait for certainty, they move with awareness, and they adjust as they go. Maybe the first step wasn't a leap. Maybe it was closing a tab, saying no, sending that email, or maybe just skipping a meeting. Maybe it didn't even feel like a step until later. That's the Rogue's way. Your momentum doesn't always look like progress, but it is. You might still hear the voice in your head that says,

"Not yet. Just wait a little longer," but there's another voice, too, quieter, the one that says: "You don't need a title, you don't need approval, and you don't need perfect clarity. You just need to start."

That's the one to listen to, and that's the one that gets you moving. There's no big ceremony, no trumpets, no fanfare. Just you and a single decision.

You just need to make it.

Street Skill: Answer the Call

A quiet move that puts you in motion. You don't need to take a leap, you just need to move.

Pick one:

- Name a decision you've been putting off because you're waiting for permission. What would it look like to make it yours?
- Choose one step you can take alone, something that doesn't require approval, applause, or backup.
- Write a single sentence that begins your journey: "I don't need _______ to start."

That's your first Street Skill.

It is quiet, intentional, but it is yours.

In the Shadows, We Learn

The Rogue isn't built in the spotlight. They're built in the background. While others speak to be heard, the Rogue listens to understand. While others perform to be seen, the Rogue studies what's real, and when the noise settles, the Rogue is the one who already knows what to do, because they've been watching.

This is what makes the Rogue dangerous, not their speed, not their charm, but their ability to move based on what others missed.

The Illusion of Visibility

We live in a world where visibility is rewarded. Being loud, being first, post more, speak faster, and take up space. That can work, but only to a point. Sometimes, the smartest person in the room is the one who isn't rushing to speak. The Rogue understands this. They know that being seen doesn't always mean being respected, and just because you're quiet doesn't mean you're not in control. You can gather more intel in two minutes of watching than most people do in an hour of talking. So while others are busy trying to be seen, the Rogue is studying how things actually work. I didn't know it back then, but I was already living this.

When I was younger, I played baseball. I wasn't a big sports fan, but my mom insisted I join to meet friends. I complained every year, but looking back, I'm glad I played. It taught me more than I realized. I wasn't the loud one. I didn't heckle, shout, or try to intimidate the other team like most kids did. Instead, I watched, and I would pay attention to how the other players moved. The way certain pitchers telegraphed their throws. The rhythm of a batter's stance. The tells before a steal. I turned every strikeout into data. Their windup became a telegraph, their stance, a code. By the 7th inning, I could predict pitches like a cardsharp spotting marks.

Did I want to win? Of course. What kid doesn't?

I didn't out-yell anyone. I tried to out-see them. I didn't know it then, but that way of watching would shape how I moved through work, relationships, and pressure later in life.

The Power of the Background

Rogues thrive at the edge of the room, the back of the meeting, the still corner of the group chat. These are not places of weakness. They're vantage points.

From the background, you learn people's tells. Who's performing, who's connecting, who's trying too hard to hold the room. You can tell who's talking to impress versus who's talking to connect. You notice patterns, body language, tone, timing, tension. You see who holds real influence and who's just trying too hard to fake it. It's not magic, it's attention. The kind most people never develop because they're too focused on being noticed. The Rogue watches everything, and when it's time to move, they move with information, not impulse.

It's the same reason a scout climbs a tree before making a move. Distance doesn't mean detachment, it means perspective. From the edge, you see the entire board. From the background, you spot the cracks before they spread.

You're not hiding, you're positioning.

The Rogue doesn't need to be the center of attention. They're too busy reading the room the way others read headlines.

Real-World Rogue Sensing

This isn't fantasy. You've seen this play out in real life. This kind of presence shows up in meetings, in classrooms, in relationships, the ones who see the shift before it's spoken, the risk before it's obvious.

Keanu Reeves isn't loud. He doesn't chase headlines or dominate interviews. When he moves, when he speaks, signs onto a project, or just sits still, people pay attention. He's built influence through restraint. He's become iconic by not playing the game. He doesn't demand the spotlight. He controls it by knowing when to step into it.

Let's look at **Angela Bassett**. One of the most respected actors alive, not because she's always on, but because she's deliberate. She listens, she waits, and she shows up with precision. She turns every scene, every moment, into a masterclass. Not by outshouting, but by out-reading everyone around her.

Both of them move like Rogues. Not loud, not flashy, but undeniable. That's not charisma. That's a presence earned through awareness, and presence starts with observation.

I see this every day with my wife.

She doesn't need to dominate a room. She walks in measured, confident, calm. She notices what others miss. The shifts in energy, unspoken tension, and what people say without saying it. She doesn't guess, she understands. Sometimes, I swear she has the mind of a wizard but the skills of a Rogue. She watches, listens, absorbs, and when she moves, it's always with precision.

She doesn't force attention. She earns it, because her presence speaks louder than volume ever could.

Rogue work doesn't demand attention. It earns respect in silence.

How to Watch Like a Rogue

This isn't just about noticing surface-level things. It's about developing situational awareness, something most people never train. Observation builds your timing. Every move you make is only as sharp as what you noticed before it.

Start with this:

- In your next meeting, watch who talks first versus who gets listened to.
- In social settings, observe who others gravitate toward and who they avoid.
- When someone's venting, listen not just to their words, but to what they're avoiding saying.

Notice tension shifts. Changes in tone, eye contact, who holds it, and who breaks it. You're not judging. You're learning. This is Rogue intel and the more you gather, the more precisely you can move.

In some games, characters have a perception score that shows how much they notice, even when they're not actively looking. The sharpest ones aren't lucky, they're just always paying attention. Rogues tend to have a high perception, not because of magic or luck, but because they're always reading the room. In real life, it works the same way. You build your perception by choosing to pay attention when others tune out. By training yourself to observe the table before making your move. By reading the vibe before raising your voice.

The Rogue's greatest moves don't come from rolling high. They come from reading right.

Observation Isn't Waiting

Let's be clear. This isn't about hiding. This isn't about staying quiet because you're afraid to speak. It's about choosing to stay quiet because you're gathering power.

Observation is an action. Silence is a move. Stillness is a setup.

The Rogue doesn't need to react to everything. That's how they stay sharp. They know their energy is limited, so they spend it with intention. While others are busy trying to win the moment, the Rogue is watching the whole board. They listen twice before speaking once. They watch what's said and what's left out. They don't flinch at the first shift. When the moment comes to speak, act, or strike, they don't guess. They know.

The world may mistake your stillness for weakness. Let them.

You don't need to explain your silence. You're not retreating. You're readying.

Street Skill: Watch and Learn

A deliberate scan reveals what others miss.

This isn't about zoning out or playing it safe. This is about choosing to notice what no one else is paying attention to. There's a certain electricity in observation. The hum of the room before anyone speaks. The flicker of discomfort when a question lands wrong. The small tells that give away tension, power, or truth. When you learn to watch like a Rogue, the world stops being chaotic and starts becoming readable. You begin to see the rhythm beneath the noise. And suddenly, you're not behind. You're ten steps ahead.

Choose one:

- Think of a recent conversation where you said little. What did you notice that others didn't?
- Pick a place you usually feel overlooked. Next time, lean into it. What patterns emerge when you're quiet?
- Observe a group, meeting, or social setting this week without inserting yourself. What power shifts can you identify?

You don't need to leap into action. Just tune in, let observation be the only move you make this week and see what changes.

This isn't hiding. This is sharpening.

The Disadvantage Advantage

"Let them think you're harmless. That's when you're most dangerous."
— The Whisper from the Shadows

Being underestimated can hurt. Being overlooked can feel personal. Being misunderstood can make you question your worth. For the Rogue, these things aren't dead ends. They're data, potential leverage, and eventually, they become an advantage.

You don't have to start with power, influence, or approval. You just need to recognize what the world is trying to use against you and decide you're going to use it better.

The Hidden Asset of Being Overlooked

The world is quick to dismiss people for being too quiet, too soft, too weird, too much, even not enough. Most people either try to overcorrect or they shut down. The Rogue does something different. They keep watching, they stay sharp, and while no one is looking, they build something no one saw coming.

Invisibility isn't failure. It's freedom. Freedom to learn, adjust, and sharpen yourself without the pressure of being watched.

No one sees you coming because they weren't watching you in the first place.

Underestimation Creates Leverage

It's a strange kind of gift when people assume you are harmless. They reveal more, guard less, and underestimate you until it's too late to adjust. The Rogue doesn't waste energy trying to convince people of their value. They let the moment do the talking.

A sharp move, done quietly, lands harder than hours of trying to prove your worth. Let people think you're not a threat.

That is their mistake to make.

Misunderstood = Unpredictable

One of the Rogue's greatest tools is being misunderstood. Not in a poetic, tortured way, just in the simple fact that people can't pin you down. When they can't define you, they can't predict you.

That kind of mystery becomes power. It gives you room to maneuver, to experiment, to evolve. You're not stuck performing one identity just to stay accepted. Being misunderstood isn't always comfortable.

It can feel lonely. It can feel unfair.

Over time, it creates a kind of internal independence that most people never develop. You get used to moving without applause. You learn to trust your read of the room before theirs.

From Outcast to Observer

In middle school, I didn't belong to any group. I wasn't popular. I didn't have the right clothes or the right body. Others made fun of me, brushed me off, and mostly ignored me. That kind of silence stays with you.

At first, I felt alone and after a while, I started to believe it. Like maybe something really was wrong with me. I'd walk into class and conversations would stop. It felt like all eyes were on me, and I knew the whispers were about me.

"Oh look, the fat kid's arrived." "Do you think he eats everything in his house to get that big?" "I wonder if he even showers."

They said it in whispers, but not quiet enough.

One day, a kid marked my arm with a Sharpie just to see if it'd still be there the next day, to "prove" whether or not I'd showered. For the record? I showered *every* day. Kids that age think those kinds of things are funny. Spoiler: it's never funny. Not for anyone. There was a stretch where I started sleeping, or pretending to, just so I wouldn't have to deal with the noise. It was easier to disappear than to listen to myself being erased out loud. Over time, something unexpected happened.

I started noticing things.

Since I wasn't caught up in the noise of trying to fit in, I started to really *see* people. I saw how the social circles worked. Who followed who, who performed, who stayed quiet and why. By high school, I wasn't part of any one clique, but I had connections across them all. I wasn't trying to fit in anymore. I was figuring people out. I never forgot what it felt like to be on the outside. That feeling never fully goes away, but what changed was how I carried it.

I stopped seeing it as a flaw. It became my advantage.

Turning Rejection Into Strategy

Everyone has experienced shame about something. Your background, your personality, your appearance, your silence. At some point, you were probably told to fix it. To get louder, or quieter, to conform. The Rogue knows something others forget. The things that get you dismissed early on often become the sharpest tools in your kit. You just need to learn how to carry them differently.

That quietness? It taught you to listen. That rejection? It taught you resilience. That weirdness? It made you creative. That anger? It made you focused.

The Rogue path is about turning the very things that made you feel less-than into weapons of clarity, strategy, and strength.

Famous Outcasts Who Rewrote the Story

Adam Savage, best known as the co-host of *MythBusters*, was not seen as traditionally "successful" early on. He bounced between interests and was told that he lacked discipline. What others called scattered, he called curious. Eventually, that same curiosity became his lockpick. His ability to blend science, creativity, performance, and engineering made him into one of the most visible educators of applied experimentation. Adam wasn't trying to be a star, he was trying to understand the world. The public caught up to him later.

Then there's **David Bowie**. When he first emerged, no one knew what to make of him. He was too theatrical, too strange, too fluid. He didn't fit into a single genre, and critics tried to dismiss him as a gimmick. Bowie didn't argue. He created. He changed identities, styles, and sounds with intention. The thing they mocked him for became the thing he mastered. He used the discomfort he caused as part of his art. He let that misread become mystique, and eventually he wasn't chasing culture. He was shaping it.

What connects them isn't perfection. It's misalignment. It's how they were written off and how their edges didn't fit the frame others tried to place them in. They studied, they experimented, they built themselves into something those early critics could no longer reach.

That's the real Rogue move.

You don't need everyone to get you and you don't need the whole room to agree. You just need to keep learning in the dark, sharpening what others overlook, and letting your path take shape in silence. The edge you carry might not look like much to others. In your hands, it becomes a weapon.

You're not behind.

You're building something they can't stop, even if they never saw it coming.

Street Skill: Flip the Script

What they dismiss becomes your edge.

Choose one:

- Think of a time you were underestimated or dismissed. What advantage did that actually give you?
- List three things you've seen as disadvantages. What skills or instincts did they force you to develop?
- The next time someone overlooks you, don't correct them. Just observe. What did they reveal by assuming wrong?

Your power isn't what they see. It's what they miss. Let them underestimate you. That's how you move past them.

They saw a disadvantage. You saw the opening.

Stealth Mode Activated

You've seen the power of being underestimated, of moving without being seen. Now it's time to learn how to use that space, not just to survive, but to control the pace of the game.

In games, stealth lets Rogues bypass traps unseen. In life? It lets you bypass noise. You're not disappearing. You're gathering information, protecting your energy, choosing when to show up and how hard to hit.

Stealth isn't hiding. It's discipline. Stealth isn't withdrawal. It's a temporary posture you choose when timing matters more than speed.

Once you learn to use it, you'll realize the most dangerous person in the room is often the one saying the least.

Stealth Is Not Hiding. It's Strategy

There's a difference between being quiet because you're afraid and being quiet because you're watching. Most of us learned early to stay small to avoid conflict, criticism, or exposure. With time and experience, that same silence becomes something else entirely. It becomes tactical.

Chosen.
Controlled.

That's the shift from survival silence to strategic restraint.

That shift doesn't happen overnight. It starts with awareness, the moment you catch yourself staying quiet, not out of fear, but because you're watching. It's subtle, but that realization changes everything. You're no longer avoiding. You're calculating.

The Rogue doesn't withhold because they have nothing to say. They wait because they know when it will matter most. They're not trying to disappear, they're deciding where they'll hit hardest.

Take the coworker in the office who used to jump into every meeting, trying to prove they belonged. They spoke fast, filled space, chased approval in every comment. Over time, something shifted. Now? They speak only when it matters. Their silence isn't hesitation, it's control. They trained themselves to listen first, to read the room, to wait for when others have emptied their noise and they can cut through it with precision. They no longer need to prove their value. They know it, and because of that, when they speak, people don't just hear them.

They *listen*.

Stillness Is a Power Move

In chaos, the Rogue stays calm.

Stillness doesn't mean freezing or doing nothing. It means choosing not to react, especially when everyone else is scrambling for control. It's in that pause that you learn what's really happening. Who's flailing, who's bluffing, and who's about to give themselves away.

Think of the father in a busy, talkative home. He doesn't need to shout to lead. He listens more than he speaks, and when he does speak, it's with care, not control. His presence isn't loud, but it's steady. The kind of calm that holds the room together. The kids may not always notice it, but they feel it, and that's what makes it powerful.

Picture the student who stood at the front of the class, someone known for keeping to themselves, never one to speak up. No slides, no notes, just quiet. At first, no one expected much. A few people barely looked up, and then they spoke. Just three clear sentences. Steady, thoughtful, exact, and the room shifted. It wasn't the length of her talk that landed. It was the weight of it. No filler, no rambling, just truth, delivered with calm precision. Presence isn't about being the loudest. It's about speaking when it counts, and when no one sees it coming, it hits even harder.

This is what we trained for in the shadows. It lets you stay centered when others spiral. It makes space for truth to rise and when you act, the timing lands with surgical precision.

Stop Leaking Your Power

You can't master stealth if you're constantly leaking energy. Every time you over-explain, over-apologize, or react too fast, you're giving something away. Most of the time, it's unnecessary. You might not even notice where you're leaking power.

It doesn't always look dramatic. Sometimes it's subtle:

- Saying yes to things just to avoid discomfort
- Explaining your boundaries more than once
- Jumping to respond in texts or emails out of anxiety
- Apologizing for having needs
- Talking longer because you're afraid of silence

The Rogue learns to control output. Not because they don't care, but because they know how much energy it takes to stay sharp.

There was this freelancer who used to pour everything into every pitch, long-winded emails, and over-detailed project plans. Talking themselves into corners because they didn't know when to stop. Now? Their process is stripped down. They send a simple, confident outline, lets the client speak, and asks a sharp question. Then they just let the silence stretch.

Before:
"I really think I'd be a great fit for this. Here's everything I can do. Let me know your thoughts!"

After:
"Here's the direction I'd recommend. What's your take?"

That shift didn't just land more clients. It saved them energy for what actually mattered.

That's what energy discipline looks like. Say less, do less, waste less, and watch your results grow louder than your words ever could.

Building Trust Through Restraint

People don't always trust the loudest voice. They trust the one who speaks with weight. The Rogue knows that reputation isn't built on visibility, it's built on consistency, timing, and precision.

Think of the nurse in a high-pressure ER. The kind who's seen more than most people could handle. He doesn't shout to be heard, and he doesn't need to prove himself. He moves through the noise with practiced calm, taking in details others miss, tracking every shift in the room. He's been through long nights, impossible choices, and moments where seconds mattered. His steadiness wasn't something he was born with. It was earned, one crisis at a time. When he speaks, it's clear and direct. People don't just hear him, they listen, because they know he isn't guessing. He's not offering noise. He's offering clarity. In the middle of the storm, he doesn't take control with force. He does it with a presence shaped by experience, held by instinct, and trusted by everyone around him.

This is the power of restraint. It builds reliability, and when people know your words are earned, they'll lean in instead of tuning out.

You don't have to fight to be heard. You just have to speak like it matters.

Let Silence Do the Work

Silence isn't a pause in the conversation. It *is* the conversation.

In negotiation, silence creates space, and space creates discomfort. Discomfort makes people talk. The more they talk, the more they reveal.

Most people can't sit with uncertainty. They rush to fill the gap with concessions, justifications, even contradictions. The Rogue doesn't chase noise. They wait. They *listen*.

In conflict, silence becomes a mirror. You don't need to argue to win. Sometimes the smartest move is the pause, the kind that makes the other person hear what they just said.

I once had a friend who always defended themselves. Every disagreement turned into a 20-minute monologue. Then they stopped. They let the silence stretch and something strange happened: people backed off, or apologized, or started talking so much they exposed the truth themselves.

Silence is a tactic, and most people walk right into it.

Moving With Intention

This is where stealth becomes movement. The Rogue doesn't stumble forward. They move on purpose.

Quietly.
Cleanly.
Confidently.

You don't have to make announcements or ask for applause. You just have to act with clarity and trust that the impact will echo, even if no one sees it coming.

Think of someone pivoting careers. They aren't tweeting about it, not building a brand, just learning new tools, connecting with key people, applying behind the scenes. Then one day they post: "Excited to start this next chapter." People are shocked, but they didn't see the hundreds of quiet steps that made it happen.

That's Rogue motion.

Not fast, not loud, but relentless and intentional.

When Stealth Isn't the Move

Let's be real. Stealth isn't the answer every time. There are moments when silence serves no one. When your voice breaks the cycle. When restraint becomes avoidance. When you need to speak up, call it out, or lead loudly.

I remember one of those moments.

At an office job I once held, there was a meeting where someone threw another team under the bus to dodge accountability. I'd been quiet most of the session, just taking notes, but something in me snapped. I spoke up, not with volume, but with clarity. I laid out the facts, dismantled the deflection, and said what no one else wanted to say. The room froze. Not because I shouted, but because no one expected it from me. That's when I realized stealth isn't silence, it's quiet momentum. You hold back so that when it matters, you hit with truth.

Not noise.

Most people burn out from trying to be heard all the time. The Rogue trains for something different. They wait, they watch, they conserve, and when the time comes to speak, they don't flinch.

So if you're ever wondering when to break the silence? It's the moment when staying quiet means losing something important. Something like your values, your voice, or your people. That's when you draw your blade.

You've trained for this.

You haven't exhausted yourself performing every moment before it. You've built your power in silence. You've honed your voice in the shadows. Stealth isn't about playing small. It's about playing smart. So when you finally step out of the quiet?

They feel it.

Let Them Wonder

The Rogue doesn't rush to correct every misread. They don't waste time explaining what they've already decided.

Let people assume. Let them fill in the blanks. Let them wonder what you're doing and why you're so quiet.

You don't owe them the commentary, just the results. You'll see it happen.

Someone writes you off, talks over you, assumes you're not ready or not serious. They move on, thinking you're out of the game.

Good.

While they're watching someone louder, you're making moves they'll never see coming. You're mapping exits, tightening plans, sharpening edges. Let them underestimate you, because by the time they realize you're a threat, it's too late. When those results show up, quiet, clean, undeniable, that's when they'll get it.

The silence wasn't you fading.

It was you sharpening.

Street Skill: Stay Sharp, Stay Quiet

Stealth isn't silence. It's intention.

This week, you move like stealth is a skill set. Not avoidance, intention.

Pick one:

- In your next conversation, wait five full seconds before responding. Just once. Let the air shift.
- Notice where you usually over-explain. Cut the filler. Let your words land without padding.
- Make a move. Career, personal, or creative, that you don't announce. Just take the step. Let others find out after.
- Watch a conversation you're not part of. Notice not just what's said, but what's avoided. What fears or insecurities are being masked by noise?

You're not hiding. You're honing. Let them wonder.

The world will try to fill your silence. Let it. Then decide what deserves your voice.

Tools of the Trade

"A rogue's power isn't in their hands. It's in what they choose to carry."
— The Whisper from the Shadows

Rogues don't win by brute force. They win because they carry less, but carry right. While others drag around clutter, physical, mental, digital, the Rogue moves with precision. Everything they carry is chosen, earned, and useful to them.

When it's time to move, they move fast, because they're not slowed down by baggage that doesn't serve them. A Rogue's toolkit isn't flashy, it's functional. It doesn't exist to impress. It exists to move.

You've learned how to observe. How to use underestimation as leverage. How to move with stealth and restraint.

Now it's time to equip yourself with habits, systems, and tools that make those moves faster, sharper, and lighter.

Thinking like a Rogue is one thing, but moving like one? That's where the real shift begins.

The Rogue's Rule: Pack Light

A Rogue never carries more than they need. Tools aren't collected for comfort. They're chosen for the moment, then set down when the moment passes.

The world wants to weigh you down. More apps, more gear, more advice, more pressure, but bulk slows you. Bloat blurs your instincts, and noise numbs the edge you've earned. That's why the Rogue kit is minimalist by design. You don't hoard, you hone. What you don't carry is as important as what you do. You don't move smarter by doing more. You move smarter by *carrying less, better.* The right tools don't make you stronger. They make you simpler.

Focused.
Fast.
Adaptable.

If it doesn't serve your next move? Discard it.

Tool #1: The Lockpick – Adaptive Learning

A Rogue doesn't carry 100 keys for 100 doors. They master the lockpick.

This is the tool that opens more than it was designed for. The flexible skill. The quick-study mindset. The Rogue doesn't know everything. They just know how to learn what they need, when they need it.

In real life, your lockpicks might be:

- Storytelling that helps you pitch, interview, or lead
- Rapid research that lets you solve on the fly
- Emotional intelligence that reads tension and timing

- Curiosity that makes complex things simple
- A lockpick mindset separates the overwhelmed from the unstoppable.

Example: Learn one skill in 20 minutes today (e.g., Excel pivot tables, a 3-part storytelling formula, how to send a cold DM). Don't master it, just pick the lock.

"A lockpick is useless if you don't listen for the click. Learn to adapt, not memorize."

Tool #2: The Smoke Bomb—Exit Strategies

The Rogue always has a way out, not because they're afraid, but because they're aware.

The smoke bomb is misdirection. A redirect. Not a retreat, but a reset. It buys you space when things get chaotic and lets you walk away without a trace of panic.

It's not cowardice. It's control.

In real life, smoke bombs are:

- A 2-line phrase that ends a draining conversation
- A financial cushion that lets you exit a toxic job
- A polite pivot when someone tries to drag you into drama
- An email draft that lets you say "no" without apology

A good exit doesn't always mean escape. Sometimes it means making sure you walk, not get dragged.

Example: Draft a one-line phrase you can keep in your back pocket.

Something like:

"That's not something I have the capacity *for right now, but I appreciate you reaching out."*

Smoke isn't for hiding. It's for redirecting attention so you can slip toward what matters.

Tool #3: The Poison Vial—Precision Strikes

The poison vial is subtle. Surgical. It's not about force, it's about patience. Placement. A single drop in the right spot that changes the outcome. This is how the Rogue turns small moves into major shifts.

In your real-world kit, this might look like:

- One carefully crafted message that cuts through the noise
- A perfect response in a moment that matters
- Sending one high-impact pitch instead of 100 mediocre ones
- Choosing not to react, then delivering one clear, confident sentence that shifts the energy

Example: Instead of sending 100 résumés, research one key hiring manager and craft a 3-sentence email that references their recent project.

"Poison isn't about force. It's about patience and placement."

Tool #4: The Grappling Hook—Leverage

When a Rogue climbs, they don't muscle their way up. They scan the wall. Find the crack. Anchor in. That's what leverage is, using what already exists to climb higher, faster, cleaner.

Leverage doesn't ask, "What don't I have?" It asks, "What haven't I used yet?"

In life, this means:

- A relationship you haven't tapped yet
- A system or platform you're under-using
- A piece of work you can repurpose or refine instead of starting from scratch
- A lesson you've learned but haven't applied

Example: Text a contact today with a specific ask. Use the tool you forgot you had.

"The best climbers don't rely on strength. They find the cracks no one else sees."

Tools Don't Make the Rogue

The gear isn't what makes you dangerous. It's how you use it. How you move with it. How you refuse to be burdened by things that don't serve your mission. A Rogue's power isn't in their inventory. It's in their intention.

You've sharpened your instincts. You've learned to move with clarity, precision, and silence. Now, your tools are just an extension of that. Not your identity, your kit.

Choose them. Carry them. Use them.

Then drop what's dead weight.

"Tools don't make the Rogue. The Rogue makes the tools."

I work in tech, and at one point I had dashboards for everything. Notion,

Asana, Excel Sheets, Slack bots. If it existed, I had a tab open for it. I thought having more tools made me sharper, more "efficient."

It slowed me down.

Not just in clicks or loading times, but mentally. I was scattered. Every system had its own rules, and I spent more time updating trackers than actually making progress. I'd open a tab to check one thing and lose thirty minutes managing the system that was supposed to save me time. Eventually, I stripped it all down. One Notion dashboard, four tabs, a couple tags, and that was it. Suddenly, I was moving faster, cleaner, lighter. Less friction. Less fatigue. I wasn't juggling tools anymore. I was executing. I stopped trying to carry every system and focused on just the ones that worked. The ones that helped me move.

Rogues don't carry clutter. They carry leverage.

Street Skill: Build Your Kit

Move like someone who doesn't carry junk, just what counts.

Choose one tool and put it into action:

- **Lockpick:** Learn one skill in 20 minutes that opens multiple doors. Could be software, storytelling, outreach, or conflict navigation.
- **Smoke Bomb:** Draft a 2-line exit phrase for a conversation or situation that drains you.
- **Poison Vial:** Cut three low-impact tasks. Replace them with one precise action with real effect.
- **Grappling Hook:** Text a contact today with a specific ask. Use the resource you already have but haven't tapped.

Pick your tool. Use it once. See what shifts. You're not adding weight. You're upgrading your edge.

Your kit is sharp. Now it's time to see what others miss. You're not packing light to look sleek, you're packing light to move sharp.

II

The Lookout

The Cutpurse survives. The Lookout starts to see.

Once you've learned to move quietly, the next step is learning where to move and when. This part is about sharpening your perception. It's about reading tension, sensing shifts, and knowing how to act without being asked. Strategy begins before anyone speaks. Clarity forms in the background.

The world rewards the loudest voice. The Rogue sharpens the quietest thought. This is where foresight becomes movement.

The Art of the Skill Check

In games, a skill check isn't about perfection. It's about one thing. Can you
do this well enough *right now*?

Life works the same way.

Rogues don't win because they max out one stat. They win because they're
skilled enough in many and know when to act. This is the art of the skill
check. Not waiting until you're perfect, just being ready when it matters. A
skill check isn't about luck. It's when preparation, awareness, and timing are
tested.

Rogues Don't Specialize, They Stack

Most people are told to find their one thing, their niche, their specialty.
Rogues don't play that game. They spread points across just enough stealth,
persuasion, and insight to slip through whatever's in front of them.

Imagine a Rogue's character sheet, the page that lists their skills, tools, and
traits in a game. Nothing is maxed out or perfect, but everything is solid.

They're not the strongest, fastest, or smartest, but they're good at a little bit of everything. That's their edge. They're never locked out of an opportunity. Whatever the situation, they've got just enough to make a move.

Specialization builds walls.
Stacking builds doors.

In real life, this looks like:

- The writer who knows just enough design to build their own brand
- The manager who can lead meetings, run numbers, and read the room
- The parent who blends logistics, empathy, and diplomacy on the fly

It's not about being the best at one thing. It's about stacking skills until you're unpredictable. The world calls it "jack of all trades."

Rogues call it stacking the deck.

Specialist vs. Rogue

You've probably heard it before: pick a lane, stick to it, master one thing until the world takes notice. The Rogue? They move differently.

Here's the difference:

The Specialist:

- Digs one deep well
- Waits to be ready
- Aces one check
- Fears looking unqualified
- Prepares for the perfect moment
- Wants recognition

The Rogue:

- Digs many shallow tunnels and links them
- Moves when it matters
- Rolls decent on all of them
- Thrives on figuring it out
- Prepares to move *now*
- Wants results

The world loves specialists because they're easy to understand. Rogues? Not so much. They're slippery, adaptable, and useful in ways you don't expect, until you need them.

What a Skill Check Really Means

A skill check is never about perfection. It's about timing. About pulling from what you've got even if it's messy and seeing if it holds.

You won't always be fully prepared, and that's okay.

The Rogue doesn't freeze, waiting for permission. They move, adjust, and roll again. That's the game.

Not mastery.
Momentum.

Why Most People Never Roll

The hardest part of a skill check isn't the action. It's the fear of failure before the roll. Most people freeze not because they don't have the skill, but because they don't trust it. They wait for confirmation, for permission, for some invisible signal that says, "You're ready now."

Rogues don't wait.

They don't ask, "Am I good enough?" They ask, "Can I try something right now that might work?" That's the shift from performance to presence. From control to motion.

The Rogue stacks just enough to move, and trusts that movement will reveal what's next. That doesn't mean they never miss, it means they miss forward.

Failure isn't what stops the Rogue. Inaction is.

How I Learned to Stack the Deck

I once got hired as a pool cleaner. I had no experience, no certifications, nothing on paper that said I was the right choice, but I picked up the steps, learned the route, and got to work.

After a few weeks, I started to see the inefficiencies, the wasted time, the energy bloat. So I rewired the route, and I optimized it based on location, task type, and which pools needed the most care. I built a cleaner system in my head, and then I ran it.

Eight-hour days became six. No shortcuts. Just cleaner lines.

Eventually, they moved me to hotel pools. More structure, more rules, better pay. Not because I was the most experienced, but because I had range. I had observation, efficiency, pattern recognition, and I took a job I shouldn't have been qualified for, and I turned it into something better.

Not by knowing more. By using more of what I had.

That's a Rogue move.

Real-World Rogue Range

Think of a solo entrepreneur. They're not a master coder, marketer, or designer, but they're dangerous because they're just good enough at all three to build something solo.

That's Rogue range.

What about a YouTuber who scripts, edits, and markets their own videos? They're not Spielberg. Their stack makes them uncopyable.

Even the person on your team who isn't loud or flashy but always fills the gaps. They fix the slide deck, de-escalate the tension, or spot the thing no one else saw coming.

Now the barista, who manages a morning rush, remembers names, and handles five micro-conflicts before 9 a.m. That's not small. That's real-world Rogue range.

They're not specialists. They're stackers.

When the moment hits? They don't freeze.

Real-World Rogue Stacks

You don't need a perfect résumé or a five-year plan. You need a stack. A mix of real, usable skills that work *in the wild*.

Creative Rogue Stack: Writing + design + social timing = fast personal brand, solo launches, pitch decks that hit

Tech Rogue Stack: Basic SQL + process mapping + communication = someone who can speak human and fix systems

Leadership Rogue Stack: Emotional intelligence + time triage + listening = the teammate who always clears the fog

Service Rogue Stack: Multitasking + name recall + conflict management = the barista who calms a five-person rush and still makes you feel seen

Parent Rogue Stack: Logistics + empathy + late-night negotiation = the strategist with a diaper bag

These aren't titles, they're weapons, and they make you more dangerous than you think.

Build Your Rogue Stack

Your skill stack is your armor. Not in how deep it goes, but in how far it reaches. You don't need a title, or a certification, or 10,000 hours.

You need awareness.

What are you better at than average? What can you blend that most people never think to combine? Maybe it's tech + storytelling, listening + timing, curiosity + calm. Your stack might not look impressive on a résumé, but it works in real life. Maybe you're great at explaining things under pressure, or staying calm when others panic, or combining creativity with strategy.

That's your stack, and it's more valuable than you think. The magic is in the mix.

Mastery is fine... but mobility?

That's next-level Rogue.

Master the Check, Not the Craft

The Rogue doesn't obsess over mastery. They master the moment. When a challenge comes up, they don't say, "I'm not ready." They roll with what they've got and move.

That's the Rogue's edge. Not in being flawless, but in being flexible. In games, you only fail a skill check if you don't try.

Lookout Move: Roll With What You've Got

I want you to tap into your own Rogue stack.

Pick one:

- List five skills you already have, even if you're not a pro.
- Combine two of them to solve one current problem differently.
- Look at someone you admire. What's their mix? What's one skill you could add next?
- Watch yourself this week. Where do you solve problems in unexpected ways? That's your stack showing up. Take note.

You don't need a perfect roll, you need motion, and when the moment comes?

Roll the check.

The Rogue's edge isn't in never failing. It's in always moving.

Sneak Attack Your Goals

Loud ambition gets the attention, but quiet precision gets the result. Rogues don't chase their goals in the open. They don't hustle for likes or broadcast every move. They prepare in silence, gather information, and strike when the moment is soft, when it bends, breaks, or opens with the lightest touch.

A sneak attack isn't accidental. It's built in the dark. This chapter is about impact, not effort. It's about knowing when *not* to move, and then landing a hit so clean no one sees it coming until it's done.

Not Every Move Should Be Public

In a world that rewards performative progress, the Rogue keeps their build quiet. While everyone else shares their grind, posts their plans, and leaks momentum, the Rogue holds it. They don't announce the strike; they become it.

A move that shifts your life doesn't need a caption.

It needs timing.

A plan loses power when it becomes performance. The Rogue keeps the silence until the work can speak.

Preparation Is Power

A sneak attack looks like luck. It's actually logistics. While others scramble, the Rogue is mapping exits, testing locks, watching patterns, and loading one perfect round. They're not stalling, they're positioning. This kind of move takes patience, it takes restraint, and it takes setup.

You have to know your terrain before you cross it.
You have to know the weak spot before you aim.
Most of all?
You have to be willing to wait.

There's a different kind of tension in this phase. It's not passive. It's charged. Like a bowstring pulled taut, just waiting to release.

Rogues don't fear the wait, they load the hit inside it.

Timing > Effort

A Rogue doesn't batter down doors.

They slip through the one hinge that's loose. It's not about swinging harder, it's about swinging smarter. This is where hustle culture falls apart. Effort without aim just burns you out.

The Rogue watches for the shift, waits for the crack, and then moves with surgical timing.

That's what makes the hit land harder.

Not size.
Not speed.
Just silence and strategy.

That's why Rogues never swing blindly. They save every ounce of force for the one strike that matters.

One Sharp Hit Beats a Hundred Swings

You don't need 40 hours of "productivity" to move forward. You need one focused strike.

Instead of 50 job apps? Message one decision-maker with a tailored ask. Instead of daily content? Drop something so well-placed it starts a conversation without you in it. Instead of announcing your goal? Build it until it's real, then let the result cut through the noise.

Rogues don't waste energy.

They wait.
Then they land the hit.
Sometimes? They don't need to hit at all.

They just slip the lock and disappear before the room realizes anything's changed.

Real-World Rogues: When It's Done, Then You Strike

Reshma Saujani didn't win her run for Congress. She failed, publicly, loudly, and then she vanished. For years, she quietly scaled Girls Who Code from 20 students in 2012 to 3,000 by 2014, partnering with companies like Twitter before the media noticed. By 2018? 80,000 students. She didn't rebound. She built a backdoor into the system, not with noise, but with leverage.

Now contrast that with Donald Glover. For 12 years, he multiclassed in silence. Writing for 30 Rock at 22, starring in Community by 25, and mixtapes as Childish Gambino on the side. All the while, the industry saw him as just 'that funny guy.' Then in 2018: This Is America. No warning. Just a decade's payoff.

Two Rogues, two fields, one rule. The world only sees the strike, but never the shadows where it was forged.

Two different styles.
Same blueprint.
Both built in silence.
Both struck with timing.

They both changed the game without needing the room to clap first.

The Rogue's Setup

Before you move, ask yourself:

- Have I scouted the terrain first?
- Am I doing this to *change* something, or just to *announce* something?
- Is the timing mine, or am I rushing to match someone else's pace?
- Am I aiming for leverage, not applause?

The Rogue has no interest in chasing praise for preparation. They're saving energy for precision, because if it's not a strike.

Then it's just sweat.

Lookout Move: Strike With Precision

Don't move harder. Move smarter.

Choose one:

- Pick a goal you've talked about publicly. Now take one silent step toward it, without telling anyone.
- Make a setup list, a short checklist of what needs to be in place before you take your swing.
- Identify one ally who could quietly open a door. Don't ask yet. Just observe. Learn how they move.
- Or: Look at a past "swing" that missed. What would have made the strike land cleaner?

You don't need more force. You just need a cleaner angle.

The world remembers the strike.

The Rogue remembers the moment the blade was ready.

Cunning Action

> **"If you're still deciding, you're already late"**
> — The Whisper from the Shadows

Rogues don't wait around for perfect conditions. They don't stall under the weight of overthinking. Once they see the play, they move. And it's already too late for everyone else to catch up.

Cunning action isn't chaos. Cunning action isn't rushing. It's moving once the pattern is clear, even if the outcome isn't guaranteed.

It's clarity in motion. This chapter is about turning hesitation into decision, and decision into impact. The Rogue has seen enough.

It's time to act.

Overthinking Is a Delay Trap

Waiting feels safe. So we wait. We wait for more proof, more clarity, more certainty, more signs. All the while, the opportunity thins out or disappears entirely.

The truth?

Most of the time, we already know. We just don't want to act. Not yet. Not without permission. Not without consensus. The Rogue understands: Waiting is often just disguised fear, and fear doesn't protect your future.

It delays it.

Overthinking feels like preparation, but it's just a slow erosion.

Cunning Action = Velocity with Vision

Cunning action isn't reckless. It's **velocity with vision.** The Rogue doesn't leap blind. They leap the second the path clears.

They move fast, but only after they understand the pattern. This is the moment where instinct meets intel.

The Rogue has gathered the clues.

Now they pivot, decisively, and without hesitation. Not because they're impulsive. But because they know **hesitation kills advantage.** Every second you delay, the opening narrows.

Momentum has math. And the Rogue moves before the numbers shift.

Real-Life Rogue Moves

Think about this bakery owner.

Foot traffic started dying. While other shops clung to routine and hoped things would bounce back, they saw what was coming. They didn't wait for a committee. They rewired their business model in silence. They started a local delivery service. Launched online ordering, mobilized their regulars, and two months later, they were growing.

The others?

Shuttered.

That's cunning action: not panic, not delay. Just smart, timely motion.

Now imagine an employee stuck in a cycle. Every six months, someone promised them a promotion. Every time? Nothing. After the third cycle, they didn't wait for another broken promise. They didn't rage quit; they backdoor-pivoted before anyone saw them leaving. They just updated their résumé, made moves, and landed somewhere better before the next 'almost' could hit.

That's a Rogue reading the pattern. And acting on it.

Now picture the musician whose audience plateaued. Instead of doubling their content schedule or copying trends, they pulled back. Took a two-week silence. Then dropped one stripped-down acoustic version of a song their fans had only heard live. No fanfare. Just precision, and it tripled their engagement, not because she worked harder.

They struck when the timing was right.

How I Knew It Was Time to Go

Five years ago, I walked away from a job I'd been at for 13 years. I had moved up from rep to trainer to quality analyst. I was good, damn good. For years, they promised me a promotion to a manager.

Over and over.

Eventually, I saw it. I wasn't being set up to lead. I was being used where I was most useful. The promotion timelines kept stretching. But my workload didn't. That disconnect became too clear to ignore.

I read the pattern.

They needed me in place, not in charge. So, I started talking to a friend who had an opening at their company. Quietly, I made the call. I updated my résumé in secret. I rehearsed the notice in my head. I visualized the moment I would walk out without flinching. When I gave my notice, they told me, "You're up next. Just a few more months."

I didn't believe them. I trusted what I'd seen. And I left. It was one of the best decisions I've ever made. Because I didn't wait to be chosen.

I chose myself.

Pattern Recognition = Permission

Rogues don't wait for a sign. They read the flags and go. Three identical red flags? That's not doubt. That's data.

You don't need to journal through it for another month.
You don't need a meeting about it.
You don't need to rehearse what you already know.

If the pattern is clear, the Rogue moves.

They don't justify. They act.

Action Creates Optionality

Decisions don't close doors. They open new ones. When you hesitate, you shrink the space for motion. But when you move, even imperfectly, you get feedback.

Insight.
Options.

Rogues don't obsess over perfection. They move with what they've got, then adjust as they see more. Cunning isn't knowing everything.

It's knowing enough to start.

Rogue's Decision Filter

Ask yourself:

- Have I seen this pattern before?
- Will more time change the facts?
- What's the cost of waiting?

Three yeses?

You're not deciding. You're delaying.

Lookout Move: Move Before You're 100% Ready

Decide fast. Move sharp. Adjust later.

Choose one:

- Make a decision you've been stalling on, even if it's small. Commit. Act. Don't ask for confirmation.
- Set a 5-minute timer and decide something you've been spinning on. Clarity comes when you move.
- Write down three patterns you keep noticing. Pick the one that's cost you the most energy and cut it loose today.
- Identify one moment where you've seen enough and move on it. Not

because it's perfect. Because it's time.
- Look back at a hesitation you regret. What would you do differently next time?

The Rogue knows: **hesitation is the enemy of advantage.**

When the path clears?

Strike.

Not because you're ready.
But because they'll never see you coming.

Traps, Locks, and Escape Plans

"The trap isn't the problem. It's not seeing it until it's closed."
— The Whisper from the Shadows

Rogues don't fear traps.

They study them.

Most people wait until they're stuck, burned out, boxed in, or blindsided. The Rogue moves differently. They don't just react to danger. They *read for it*. They know that most traps aren't obvious.

They're polite.
Subtle.
Familiar.

The hard truth? Most cages don't start as prisons. They start as comfort, safe routines, familiar roles, easy praise. Over time, what once felt cozy can start to close in.

This chapter is about seeing the signs. Spotting the pressure plates and building exits before you need them. This isn't about living on guard. It's about noticing patterns early so you have choices when they appear.

The Trap Isn't Always Obvious

Not all traps snap shut. Some just slowly close around you while you're being thanked.

"You're so good at that. Can you help just this once?"
"We'd be lost without you."
"You're next in line… just give it more time."

The Rogue doesn't just listen to words. They read the shift.

If the praise is locking you into a role you didn't choose, if the promise comes with strings, if the "just for now" has no end in sight. That's not appreciation.

It's a snare with good PR.

Trap Types: The Rogue's Lexicon

The Favor Trap - You say yes once. Then twice. Then it becomes expected. Until the moment you set a boundary, you're suddenly "difficult."

Compliance becomes the price of belonging.

The Loyalty Lock - You stay in the job, the relationship, the system, because you "owe" them. Even when it no longer aligns with who you are.

Loyalty without growth becomes captivity.

The Upgrade Cage - You get the title. The recognition. The raise. But you lose time, freedom, and say-so. The promotion looks shiny until you realize the lock's on the inside.

More status, less space.

The Bait-and-Switch Snare - They promise more later, after this busy season, this quarter, this launch. But the timeline keeps moving. And the "temporary sacrifice" becomes permanent.

The reward becomes the excuse.

The Self-Sacrifice Snare - You're so used to helping others, you forget what your own needs even sound like. You're praised for being selfless until there's nothing left.

You don't notice the trap because you built it.

How I Tripped the Trap Before It Sprung

Before I started writing and teaching, I worked as a CNA. I was good at my job. I showed up every day, learned my role, and took pride in how I handled it. Eventually, the manager of the house noticed and offered me a supervisor position.

It sounded like everything you hope for. More pay, more responsibility, more recognition, but before saying yes, I paused. I evaluated what was really on the table. The raise was real. The title was real. But so was the new reality: my hours would jump from 40 a week to 70, sometimes more.

That's when I realized something important.

This wasn't an opportunity. It was a dressed-up trap. If I said yes, I would burn out. Fast. The job I once enjoyed would start to corrode from the inside out. I saw the pressure plate before I stepped on it, so I walked around it.

Saying no didn't mean losing progress. It meant protecting the part of me that could keep moving forward without being chained to someone else's timeline.

Spot the Pressure Plates

Most traps don't leap at you.

They wait.
They blend in.

Then they snap shut when you're too deep to dodge. The Rogue doesn't just react. They read the signs early:

- **Emotional tells** — resentment, dread, or that weight in your chest before a meeting
- **Social patterns** — rules that shift, expectations you didn't agree to, side-eyes for saying "no"
- **Situational loops** — the same promises, the same apologies, the same stuck conversations

A Rogue doesn't step without scanning.

The truth hides in plain sight. Every step leaves something behind.

Real-World Rogues Who Walked Free

Erin Brockovich - She wasn't supposed to matter. She had no law degree, no title, just instinct. She spotted the pattern. People in a small town getting sick, utility documents that didn't add up, and a company hiding the truth. She followed the trail and uncovered that Pacific Gas & Electric had been poisoning the local water supply for years.

Most people would've backed off. Erin didn't. She kept going.

She didn't just fight the case. She exposed the design.

The trap was legal. The escape was tactical.

Mae Jemison - made history as the first Black woman to travel to space. That milestone could have been her whole identity. Instead, after just one mission with NASA, she chose to step away. Staying would have meant staying inside the box, and she had other paths to explore.

She pivoted to art, teaching, and entrepreneurship, not out of necessity, but out of intention.

She didn't let the legacy become a leash.

Ke Huy Quan - He started as a childhood star in *The Goonies* and *Indiana Jones*, then vanished from the spotlight. It wasn't by choice. Hollywood had no room for him outside of tired stereotypes.

So he stepped back, shifted behind the scenes, and kept learning. While others forgot his name, he studied, stayed curious, and waited for a door worth walking through.

When the moment finally came, he didn't just return, he hit with precision. His performance shook the room and earned him an Oscar.

He wasn't gone. He was sharpening. That's the Rogue way.

Every Trap Has a Lock. Every Lock Has a Plan.

The Rogue doesn't ask, *"Am I stuck?"* They ask, *"Where's the exit?"*

Here's how they find it:

- **Mentally:** Detach from the identity that keeps you frozen ("But I'm the reliable one.")

- **Strategically:** Build exits before you're desperate, emotionally, financially, relationally
- **Socially:** Shift the dynamic without making a scene. Don't explain it, don't announce it, just move differently. Let your silence create space, lower the tension, and change the tempo of the room.

There's always a back door, or a way to make one.

Sometimes the lock isn't on the door. It's on the part of you that forgot you could walk away.

Locks can be picked.
Hinges can be removed.
Maps can be drawn.

The Rogue doesn't just look for open doors. They make their own exits.

Rogue's Trap-Scan Checklist

Ask yourself:

- **Does this shrink my options over time?**
- **Is there an unspoken punishment for saying no?**
- **Would walking away cost me more than staying?**

Three yeses? You're not in a situation.

You're in a *system.*

Lookout Move: Scan the Room Before You Move

Look before you leap. Listen before you trust.

Choose one:

- Name one trap you've been walking into. What's the trigger? What's the cost?
- Where are you staying out of loyalty, not alignment?
- Build a quiet exit plan this week, just in case. You don't have to use it. You just have to know it's there. (**Note**: If you're in a situation where safety is at risk, especially in cases like abuse or domestic violence, know that this advice may not apply in the same way. Those circumstances require support, not just strategy. You're not alone, and there are resources built to help.)

Rogues don't fear traps. They map them, because the most dangerous prison is the one you don't see.

Knowing there's a trap doesn't make you paranoid.

It makes you prepared.

Reading the Room

> *"Fools rush in. Rogues slip out and leave others wondering when they even left."*
> — The Whisper from the Shadows

You've learned to move with silence, strike with precision, and scan for danger before it lands. Now, the game shifts again. It's no longer just about where you are, it's about who you're with and what they don't say.

Systems have rules. People have tells and the Rogue? They read both. This chapter is about social awareness, not as a soft skill, but as a survival tool.

A quiet force.
A strategic edge.

Where You've Been: From Shadows to Sight

In **Part I**, you embraced movement, observation, and resilience. You learned to stay light. To stay quiet. To carry only what served.

In **Part II**, you added timing, decisiveness, and escape plans. You stopped reacting and started executing.

Now? You're seeing the room as terrain.

The Rogue doesn't just track systems. They track *people.*

Social Awareness Is the Rogue's Sixth Sense

This isn't about reading the vibe, it's about reading the pattern. Psychologists call it **thin slicing.** The brain's ability to make rapid, surprisingly accurate judgments based on very limited information.

In their study *"Half a Minute: Predicting Teacher Evaluations from Thin Slices of Nonverbal Behavior and Physical Attractiveness"* (published in the *Journal of Personality and Social Psychology*), Nalini Ambady and Robert Rosenthal found that people could accurately assess a teacher's effectiveness after watching just thirty silent seconds of behavior, almost as well as students who spent an entire semester with them.

Speed isn't sloppiness, speed is skill.

The Rogue doesn't rely on guesses. They hone this instinct through experience, sharpening their perception until it cuts faster and cleaner than conscious thought. They know thin slicing works best when you've seen enough patterns to recognize the real ones and avoid the traps of snap bias.

The Rogue sees:

- Who's pretending to lead
- Who's holding real leverage
- Who's about to crack
- Who's about to dominate

Words lie, body language whispers, and energy tells the truth.

Psychologists studying **nonverbal leakage,** the unconscious revealing of true emotions, confirm what the Rogue already knows. Posture, tone, microexpressions, and pauses often say more than a dozen rehearsed speeches, but even here, the Rogue moves carefully.

Not every signal is a truth. Some are shields, and some are bait.

It's the poker player who folds before the river card because of a fingertip twitch. The negotiator who senses a deal slipping away from a half-second pause. The Rogue who knows the real decision-maker isn't at the head of the table, but sitting three seats back, saying nothing.

Most people listen to what's being said.

Speak, Listen, Vanish

Speak:

- When silence would cost you influence
- When your words cut through noise, not add to it
- When your voice shifts the dynamic, not just adds heat
- When staying silent would be misread as agreement

Listen:

- When no one else is
- When conflict is spiraling
- When someone powerful chooses silence, that's when they're most alert
- When alliances are being formed quietly, not announced loudly

Vanish:

- When the cost of staying outweighs the gain of being seen
- When your exit will be noticed more than your presence
- When drama becomes the main currency in the room

- When survival is replacing solution

A Rogue never overstays their usefulness. Sometimes the sharpest presence is your absence.

Situational Mastery Is Power

You've seen it:

- The teammate who never interrupts but lands the closing word
- The quiet one who says nothing in the meeting then sends one message that realigns everything
- The leader who pauses and the room leans in

That's not luck. That's calculated presence.

That's *placement.*

You don't dominate the space. You move with intention inside of it.

Tilt the Room

Once you can read it, you can *shift* it.

The Misdirection Move
Redirect tension without confronting it.

"What would this look like if we weren't on a deadline?"

The Temperature Check
Name the thing no one's saying.

"Feels like we're stuck between X and Y, am I reading that right?"

The Echo

Paraphrase a loud voice to redirect credit or clarity.

"So what I'm hearing is, we're stuck on delivery, not direction. Right?"

The Rogue Withdrawal

Leave early, skip the room entirely, not to disappear, but to *control your access.*

You don't dominate the room. You disrupt it quietly.

Lookout Move: Tune In Before You Talk

Before you move the room, let it move through you.

Choose one:

- In your next group setting, say nothing for 10 minutes. Watch. Who leads? Who follows? Who checks out?
- Think back to a recent conversation. What wasn't said but shifted everything?
- Choose one moment this week to leave early or stay silent longer than usual. Notice what changes when you *don't fill the space.*

The Rogue isn't loud. They're present with precision.

Closing the Lookout

You've learned to read systems. Now you're reading people. Next? You'll learn to read *yourself.* To know when to show your face or when to wear the mask, and when to let them underestimate you. *On purpose.*

Part III isn't about hiding, it's about how to let them see only what you choose.

The final Rogue skill? Controlling the narrative.

They ask, *"Where did you go?"*

You smile. *"Where didn't you look?"*

III

The Shadow

The Lookout watches. The Shadow learns to choose what to reveal. Once you've learned to see the game, you have to decide which part of you plays it. This part is about masks, myths, and the moments you realize not every door is worth unlocking. Rogues are mistaken for loners, but this isn't solitude. It's precision. It's protection.

The world shows its profile.
The Rogue chooses their reflection.
This is where control becomes identity.

The Mask You Wear

> **"Blend in long enough, and you'll forget what your real voice sounds like."**
> — The Whisper from the Shadows

Everyone wears a mask. The Rogue's question isn't if, it's why.

Masks protect.
They filter.

They help us navigate rooms that don't feel safe, roles we didn't choose, and expectations we never agreed to, but over time, the mask sticks, the role hardens, and eventually, if you're not paying attention? You lose the shape of your real face.

Everyone Wears a Mask

You don't owe every room the same version of you. That's not deception, it's strategy.

A mask can let you pass through unseen.
In some moments, it keeps the peace.
In others, it buys you space to think before you act.

If you stop recognizing it as something you *put on*, it becomes something that *defines you,* and the longer it stays on, the harder it is to remember what's underneath.

The Roles We Get Trapped In

Some masks are handed to us, and some we create to survive, but either way, the danger is the same. They become habit.

- The fixer who's never allowed to break
- The quiet one who gets talked over until they stop trying
- The strong one who's never offered help
- The peacemaker who sacrifices their own needs
- The "low-maintenance" one who never asks for anything, even when they're drowning
- The reliable one who never drops the ball, even when it's too heavy
- The self-starter who always figures it out alone and forgets they're allowed to ask for help
- The adaptable one who becomes what every room needs, until they forget what *they* need

They're roles that are familiar, useful, even praised. They become traps when they cost you presence, power, or peace.

> "The longer you wear their mask, the tighter it fits."
> — *The Whisper from the Shadows*

Camouflage vs. Signal

There's a difference between hiding and choosing.

Camouflage is how you blend in when needed. To pass unnoticed, reduce threat, or move cleanly.

Signal is how you stand out. How you show who you are, where you stand, and who should come closer (or back off).

Rogues know how to use both, but they always know which one they're doing. Camouflage keeps you safe, while signal draws allies or lines. It only becomes dangerous when you stop choosing, when your mask becomes your only face.

Sometimes, blending saves you. Like the first week at a new job, when everyone's talking, but you're watching the real power lines. There are moments when, signaling changes everything. Maybe it's the quiet nod to someone who's drowning in the room and letting them know they're not alone.

Rogues move between both. By choice, not by default.

Strategic Presentation (Not Performance)

This isn't about being fake. It's about being *intentional*.

Some rooms deserve restraint.
Some don't deserve your energy at all.

Here's the question that cuts:

- Is your silence strategy or surrender?
- Are you watching the room or shrinking into it?
- Are you flexible or disappearing?
- Are you choosing the mask or letting it wear you?

Rogues don't perform. They position, but when performance becomes your personality, and you forget you're performing. That's when the mask stops protecting you and starts replacing you.

When to Drop the Mask

You don't have to show your full self in every room, but you do need to know when the mask is costing you more than it protects you.

Drop the mask when:

- It keeps you from growing
- It costs you your values
- It makes you invisible to the people who need to really see you
- When the person in the mirror starts feeling like a stranger

The Rogue doesn't give everything away, but they never lie to themselves.

The Mask I Wore

For most of my life, I wore the mask of the peacekeeper, the mediator, the one who smoothed things over.I calmed people down and held the tension no one else wanted to touch.

It wasn't a role I chose. It was one handed to me.

I wore it so well that I started to believe it was who I really was, and for a long time, it worked. I kept the peace. I made people feel safe, but the cost? That showed up quietly. Like the way I bit my tongue when I disagreed, the way I stayed in rooms longer than I should have, the way I said "it's fine" when it wasn't.

I remember one fight, not loud, just… cold. I let someone walk all over my boundaries because I didn't want to make things worse. So I just said nothing. Later, they thanked me for being "so understanding." That moment hit differently. It wasn't me being understanding. I was disappearing.

That's when I realized what the mask had taken.

As I got older, I began to see it for what it was. A mask of expectation, not identity. I didn't realize how much I had silenced in myself to make room for others until I finally took it off. Taking the mask off didn't make everything easier. Some relationships shifted. A few ended. What stayed, though, were the ones built on something real. People who actually knew me.

I still wear that mask sometimes, but now I know it's a mask. That means I get to decide when and if it goes back on.

Shadow Work: Inventory the Masks

Know the mask. Choose the mask. Drop the mask.

Choose one:

- List three roles you tend to play in different rooms. Which ones serve you? Which ones are starting to drain you?
- Think of a time you held back a part of yourself to keep the peace. What did it cost you?
- This week, choose one interaction where you'll show up a little less filtered. Watch how it changes the room and how it changes you.

Remember: this is your mask, on your terms. You don't owe anyone your full identity, but you do owe yourself the freedom to choose what you show and when.

Masks aren't weaknesses. They're tools. You're just learning when to set them down, and when to wear them like armor, on your terms.

The Rogue's truth isn't hidden. It's revealed when they're ready.

Not Every Chest Is Worth Picking

Rogues love a locked door, but masters? They love walking away from the wrong one. The thrill of the pick, the challenge, the mystery, the possibility is intoxicating. If you're not careful, you start opening every chest just because you *can*.

You burn time, energy, focus, chasing every shiny opportunity.

You say yes to jobs you don't want, partnerships you can't maintain, and plans that were never yours to begin with, and somewhere in the middle of all that motion?

You trap yourself in someone else's idea of success.

The Art of Discernment

Discernment is what separates the skilled from the smart.

It's the difference between knowing *how* to pick a lock and knowing when it's not worth the time.

Before you say yes, ask:

- Is this mine to open?
- Do I want what's inside?
- Would I still choose this if no one ever saw me do it?
- What would it *cost* me to say yes?

The world praises "go-getters."

The Rogue isn't trying to get *everything*. They're trying to get what fits. What aligns. What sustains, because every yes has a cost, and not every chest holds treasure.

I used to keep trying to pick the same lock, year after year. Thirteen years at the same job. I showed up, improved, led quietly, and waited. They promised a promotion. Then another. Then another. It always seemed close. Just one more quarter, one more restructure, one more budget cycle.

At first, I told myself it was loyalty. That I was earning something. That staying meant something. But deep down, I knew the truth: I wasn't stuck because I couldn't grow. I was stuck because I kept hoping the door would open if I just kept turning the key.

I didn't just waste time. I started to shrink. I pulled back from the things I loved. My momentum faded, my voice got quieter. I stopped building, stopped risking, and I told myself I was being patient, careful, strategic. What I was really doing… was waiting for permission.

Permission to matter.
To try.
To fail and still belong.

One day, I stopped asking what I was waiting for and started asking what it was costing me. The answer was hard to face, but honest. So I stopped hesitating. I picked a path. Not because it was safe, but because it moved. It wasn't easy, but it was mine.

That was the first time I truly understood. Just because you can open a door doesn't mean it leads anywhere worth going.

Real-World Rogues Who Knew When to Walk Away

Viola Davis - Career Discernment
She could have kept collecting roles. But she started saying no. Roles that lacked depth. Characters that fit the same mold. She waited until she could say yes to parts that carried soul, nuance, and truth, even if it meant waiting longer between projects.

She didn't chase screen time, she chased substance.

Rick Moranis - Exit with Intention
He was at the top of his game. *Ghostbusters, Spaceballs, Honey, I Shrunk the Kids.* Then he walked away. No final tour, no dramatic press. He chose to raise his kids after his wife passed, stepping out of the spotlight completely.

He didn't chase relevance, he chose what mattered.

The Freelancer - Rewriting the Rules
They said yes to every client, to every collab, to every ask. Then, they burned out, fast. When they finally stopped, raised her prices, and chose clients based on values, not volume, they made more, stressed less, and stopped performing busy just to feel valuable.

They earned the difference between *busy* and *better.*

The Single Parent in School

They got offered a scholarship to a top program, but it didn't fit their schedule as a working parent. So they passed. Found a different path that honored their time, their energy, their priorities. Graduated on *their* terms.

They passed on prestige. Chose alignment.

Colin Kaepernick - Voice Over Visibility
He had a contract, a team, a career, and he took a knee. Not because it was safe, but because it wasn't. He saw a system designed to keep people quiet, and he chose to signal instead. The cost was steep: lost endorsements, lost opportunities, lost seasons. That impact echoed far beyond the field.

He didn't protect the brand. He protected his values.

When to Walk Away

How do you know the chest isn't worth it?

- You feel more *relief* at the idea of saying no than you do excitement about saying yes
- The opportunity feels urgent but only on *their* timeline
- It requires you to shrink or stay silent
- It feels like *proof*, not purpose. Like you're just trying to show you *can*

This isn't fear.
This is clarity.

What's Inside the Chest?

Sometimes the most dangerous thing about the chest... is what's *not* in it.

- No boundaries
- No alignment

- No growth
- Just a well-crafted distraction designed to keep you moving, so you don't stop to ask why

Ask yourself:

- Who benefits most if I open this?
- Who carries the consequences if it goes wrong?
- Would I still want this if no one ever praised me for it?

Some chests are glitter.
Some are traps.
Some are just empty.

The Rogue doesn't pick to prove they can. They pick to move with purpose.

Shadow Work: Discern Before You Pick

You don't need every door, just the right one.

Choose one:

- List three things you said yes to recently. Which ones were aligned? Which were driven by fear, guilt, or FOMO?
- What's one "no" you're proud of? What did it protect?
- What's one "no" you *regret*? What did it teach you?
- This week, say no to something that feels impressive, but misaligned. Use that space to find something that aligns.

Leave It Locked

You don't have to chase every lock.
You don't have to prove anything.
Knowing which chests are worth their scars is the real skill.

The Solo Class Myth

> ***"Even the lone wolf gets tired. Rogues survive longer when they know who to trust."***
> — The Whisper from the Shadows

There's a myth that clings to Rogues like shadow to steel. That they always go it alone, and that they prefer it that way.

That independence becomes part of our identity and that asking for help means you've failed the class.

It's a great story. Romantic, even. The lone blade in the dark, a shadow no one sees coming, no backup, no strings, but here's the truth. Going it alone isn't always power. Sometimes, it's exhaustion in disguise. The best Rogues? The ones who survive, not just the mission, but the whole campaign?

They're not solo, they're strategic. They know when to be invisible, and when to let someone watch their back.

The Myth of the Lone Rogue

Pop culture loves the image of the solitary operator. The gruff mercenary, the silent thief, the brooding assassin in the corner booth. Sure, sometimes we *do* work best alone, sometimes solitude is clarity, and silence is strategy.

However, if you're always solo, something's off.

Eventually, doing everything alone stops being a flex. It becomes a burden and burdens break you down.

Being a Rogue isn't about isolation. It's about autonomy, and autonomy doesn't mean you can't build trust.

It means you get to *choose* where you place it.

Why We Go Solo

Most of us don't start out this way.

We learn to go solo. We adapt to it, because somewhere along the way, the math started adding up like this:

- **Ask for help = weak**
- **Rely on someone = lose control**
- **Be vulnerable = get burned**

So we stopped asking.
We stopped hoping.
We armored up.

That armor? It gets heavy. It keeps the pain out, sure, but it keeps the good out too. The Rogue's instinct says, *"It's safer if I carry it alone."*

Instincts are shaped by wounds, and wounds don't always give great advice.

What My Wife Taught Me

For years, I carried everything myself. Didn't matter what it was, projects, stress, mistakes, weight I didn't need to hold, I'd just shoulder it.

I survived. I scraped by. I kept pushing, even when I was breaking, and yeah, I failed. More times than I'll admit, but I never reached out. Never asked for help. Not really. I just wore the struggle like armor and called it strength.

Then, I met my wife. She didn't take over. She didn't fix me. She just stood next to me.

No fanfare.
No pressure.
Just steady presence.

She showed me that letting someone in didn't make me weaker. It made everything feel lighter. I learned that trust isn't surrender, that it's a tactical decision. A move.

With that, it changed everything.

What Real Support Looks Like

Not everyone deserves access. This isn't about opening the gates wide, it's about **choosing your crew**. Real support doesn't come with noise or demands. It doesn't drain you.

It *sharpens* you.

Support can look like:

- A partner who lets you breathe without trying to take over

- A mentor who gives you the hard truths you're finally ready to hear
- A friend who checks your blind spots without making you feel small

You're still the Rogue. You're still the one making the move, but you're not the only one holding the blade.

Hayao Miyazaki & Studio Ghibli

Let's talk about Hayao Miyazaki - the legendary Japanese animator, director, and co-founder of Studio Ghibli. He's the mind behind films like *Spirited Away*, *My Neighbor Totoro*, and *Princess Mononoke*. Movies that shaped childhoods and shifted the animation world forever.

To the outside world, he's often portrayed as a lone visionary. A creative force of nature, but behind every stunning Ghibli film? There is a crew, a quiet army of artists, animators, producers, each handpicked. Each one trusted.

He protected his vision not by standing alone, but by building a team he could depend on. That's what made it work. That's what kept his voice clear. He didn't dilute his genius, he **amplified** it by knowing who to let into the circle.

That's real Rogue energy. A stealth team, not a spotlight.

Strategic Alliance vs Forced Teamwork

Let's be clear. This isn't "join a team" advice, or "make nice with everyone" fluff.

This is about **strategic alliance**.

Say *yes* to the people who:

- Respect your independence
- Help you move cleaner, quicker, deeper
- Don't create emotional debt disguised as support

Say *no* to the ones who:

- Need you to dim your light
- Drain your mana
- Pretend to be allies, but don't show up when it counts

Build your circle the same way you'd build your toolkit.

With precision and with purpose.

You Don't Have to Carry It All

The Rogue myth says you're supposed to do it alone, but the real Rogue, the seasoned one?

They know better.

You're not less powerful for letting someone in. You're more dangerous when you're supported. Rogues don't roll with crowds, but the smart ones?

They don't walk the whole path alone.

Shadow Work: Call in the Ally

Trust isn't surrender. It's strategy.

Choose one:

- Name one area of your life you're carrying alone and it's not helping

anymore
- Who could help but you haven't asked? Why?
- Ask for help this week not out of desperation, but choice
- List three people who amplify your best work and three who don't

The Rogue's code isn't silence. It's precision. You don't let everyone in, but when you do? You become something stronger than solo.

You become untouchable.

When to Dodge, When to Fight

Not every battle deserves your blade. One of the most powerful tools a Rogue has isn't the dagger or the trap, it's **discernment**.

The ability to assess a situation, fast, and decide: *Is this worth it?*

Rogues survive because they don't waste movement. They don't lash out blindly. They don't fight for ego. They strike when it matters. They disappear when it doesn't.

That's not cowardice. That's mastery.

The Rogue's Greatest Weapon: Discretion

The world will try to drag you into every drama, argument, and confrontation it can. Online. At work. In your relationships. Even in your own head. But the best Rogues know this:

Every fight costs you.

Time.
Energy.
Emotional focus.
Momentum.

Some fights sharpen you. Most just wear you down. Dodging isn't weakness, it's wisdom.

It's the art of saying, "Not today."

Why We Struggle with Boundaries

We're taught to be "the bigger person," even if it means swallowing our truth.

We're told saying no is selfish. That standing up for ourselves is "too much."

We feel guilty.
Afraid.
Unsure.

We tell ourselves:

- *If I avoid it, I'll seem weak.*
- *If I confront it, I'll ruin everything.*
- *If I stay quiet, maybe it'll pass.*

Here's the truth: **strategic boundaries aren't walls, they're filters.** They don't push people away. They keep the wrong energy from getting in.

A Rogue with no boundaries is just a target.

A Rogue with clear boundaries? Lethal.

Dodge Moves: The Art of the Exit

Sometimes the smartest thing you can do… is walk away.

Tactical withdrawal isn't losing. It's choosing not to bleed for something that isn't worth the scar.

You don't have to argue with every bad take. You don't have to explain yourself to people committed to misunderstanding you. You don't have to give access to anyone who's already shown you they can't be trusted.

Rogue Move: Silence is a decision.

There's a difference between ghosting and self-protection. Between avoidance and discernment. And you'll know the difference by the way your nervous system responds when you walk away.

Disengage from:

- Arguments that loop without resolution
- People who mistake kindness for weakness
- Cycles that keep draining your peace

You don't have to announce your exit. Just leave.

Quietly.
Strategically.
Like a Rogue.

Fight Moves: When to Strike

But some moments? Some moments call for fire.

When your values are on the line. When silence would be betrayal. When someone crosses a line that should've never been approached.

Not every fight is bad.

Sometimes the confrontation is the healing. Sometimes the boundary *is* the blade. You don't have to shout to make it count.

You just have to mean it.

> *Rogue Rule: Only unsheathe your blade if you're willing to own the consequences.*

Stand up when:

- A friend needs protection and no one else is stepping up
- You're being gaslit, manipulated, or disrespected
- The easy path would mean abandoning your integrity

Fighting clean doesn't mean going easy. It means being clear, calm, and unshakable.

Energy is Everything

Here's the truth most people miss:

You can win a fight and still lose yourself.

Every battle takes something from you. Attention, bandwidth, recovery time. The goal isn't to "win" everything. The goal is to *preserve your power*.

Before you engage, ask:

- *What's the outcome I actually want?*
- *Will this fight bring me closer to it, or just pull me into chaos?*
- *Am I fighting because I should... or because I'm triggered?*

Sometimes, the high road isn't about being noble.

It's about protecting your energy for the battles that *matter*.

The Cut and the Stand

Let me show you both sides of this.

I had a friend back in high school. We were thick as thieves, inseparable. We did everything together, as friends do. Over time, it became clear to everyone else that he wasn't really a friend. He didn't treat me well. He used me, manipulated situations, but I didn't want to see it.

For years, I ignored the signs.
Made excuses.
Told myself I was being loyal.

One day, it hit me: loyalty shouldn't cost you peace, and friendship shouldn't feel like an obligation. I didn't blow up. I didn't sink to his level.

I just... walked away.

Quiet.
Clean.

Final.

From that day on, life got lighter. I hadn't realized how much weight he brought into my world until it was gone. I stopped dreading my phone. I stopped second-guessing myself after every conversation. The tension that had lived in my chest for years started to fade.

He was my best friend for a long time, and letting go wasn't easy. Over time, I saw how much space that friendship had taken up. Space I needed for healing, for real connection, for peace.

That single decision taught me something I've carried ever since: *you don't owe everyone a fight. Sometimes, the win is in the exit.*

Not every moment calls for silence.

Anyone who knows me knows I'm easygoing. I don't get riled up easily. I try to be kind to everyone, but there are times when kindness isn't the right tool. Times when staying quiet is just another form of surrender.

In school, there was a group of kids I never got along with. I avoided them, kept my distance, did my best to stay out of their orbit. One day, they came for someone I cared about, a close friend who had always had my back. They decided he was an easy target. Mocked the way he talked, the way he walked. Laughed loud enough to pull attention. Tried to tear him down just to feel bigger.

I could've kept my head down.
Pretended not to hear it.
Told myself it wasn't my fight.

That day, I didn't.

I stepped in. Not with violence. Not with a dramatic scene. Just words. Steady, sharp, direct. I told them to stop. No threats, just truth spoken without fear. Enough to catch them off guard. Enough to make them back off.

It wasn't about being a hero. It was about not sitting in silence while someone I cared about got broken down for sport.

That moment stuck with me, because *sometimes the Rogue doesn't vanish into the shadows.*

Sometimes we step into the light, just long enough to say: *Not today.*

Shadow Work: The Boundary Check

Boundaries aren't walls. They're warning signs.

Choose one:

- List three things you're giving energy to right now that don't deserve it
- What's one situation you're avoiding that might actually need a firm boundary?
- Who tests your limits the most and what have you allowed?
- Write a one-sentence boundary you've been afraid to say out loud

Remember: boundaries are a form of clarity, and clarity is a kind of magic.

The Clean Cut

You're allowed to dodge.
You're allowed to disappear.
You're allowed to draw your line and hold it.

Not all fights are worth your blade, but the ones that are? Make them count.

The Rogue's Code

Every Rogue walks with a shadow, not just the kind cast by light, but the one shaped by memory, instinct, and experience. It trails behind every decision, shows up in the silence between moves, and waits patiently in the dark corners of the mind. For a Rogue, that shadow isn't something to fear. It's something to understand.

If the Cutpurse survives by reacting, the MasterMind thrives by knowing.

That shift starts with one thing: a code.

Not the kind written in stone or taught in school. Not rules designed by someone else to make you fit neatly into a world that doesn't quite see you. A Rogue's code is personal. Earned. Sharpened by failure, refined by reflection. It's not about being right in the eyes of the crowd. It's about being honest in the quiet of your own mind.

A Rogue moves through a world that doesn't offer many handbooks. When the rules seem bent or broken, your code is the only thing that keeps you from becoming hollow.

The Personal Compass

The world has a lot to say about what matters. Careers. Applause. Obedience. Appearances. But a Rogue doesn't live by the volume of the crowd. They live by a compass built from lived experience.

That compass may not point north, but it points true.

Maybe your code says: never betray someone who trusted you. Or finish what you start.

Maybe it's more personal. Maybe it's: speak last so you can hear more. Or don't waste time explaining yourself to people committed to misunderstanding you.

Your code doesn't have to make sense to others. It only has to make sense to you.

When I started writing this series, I didn't know if anyone would care. I didn't have a platform, a deal, or a guarantee. All I had was a compass of my own. One that said: if this helps even one person move differently, it's worth doing. And that was enough to keep going.

That's the thing about code. You don't need permission to follow it. You just need the courage to admit it's yours.

When the Crowd Isn't Right

Following your own code often means *not* following the crowd. That doesn't make you a rebel. It makes you deliberate.

Most people want belonging. That's human. Rogues know that false belonging, the kind you have to buy with silence or self-betrayal, isn't worth the cost.

There were times in my life I stayed quiet when I shouldn't have. Took a paycheck instead of a risk. Stayed in rooms where I didn't fit because I hadn't figured out how to leave. But when I started following my own code, something shifted.

I lost comfort, certainty, and approval, but I gained something better: alignment.

When you're aligned, you stop leaking energy. You stop twisting yourself into knots, trying to be what others want. You move with a clarity that doesn't need to be explained.

You just *are*.

A Rogue in the Real World

You don't have to be a thief in a cloak to live like a Rogue. Some of the most powerful code-followers walk among us quietly, people who don't brag, don't posture, and don't wait for applause. They just *live* their truth.

Prince didn't just perform music, he owned every note of it. And when the music industry tried to take control of his work, he didn't fight louder. He fought *smarter*. He changed his name to a symbol, walked on stage with the word "slave" written on his face, and outmaneuvered the system that tried to own him.

He followed a code: creative freedom above everything. He wasn't trying to please. He was trying to stay free.

He redefined what it meant to be an artist. He never waited for permission to express himself and he walked away from anything that tried to cage him.

Terry Goodkind wrote fantasy, but not the kind everyone expected. His *Sword of Truth* series was bold, direct, and unapologetically philosophical. He didn't follow genre tropes just because that's "how it's done." In fact, he resisted being called a fantasy author altogether, insisting his work was about ideas, not dragons.

He was hated for that by some, deeply respected by others, and he didn't care.

Goodkind followed a code: tell the truth, challenge assumptions, and never write for approval. His characters didn't play nice, they made hard choices. And so did he.

He once said, *"Live your own life, not someone else's idea of what your life should be."*

That's a Rogue's truth if I've ever heard one.

Shadow Work: Making Peace With the Hidden You

We all have a shadow. Not the cartoon kind. The real one. The part of ourselves that carries our fear, shame, doubt, and hidden power.

Shadow work is the Rogue's secret art. Because unlike others who ignore the darker parts, the Rogue turns toward them. Studies them. Learns from them.

The time you lied because it felt safer. The time you stayed small to be liked. The time you broke your own code to be accepted.

The Rogue doesn't bury those moments. They examine them.

And in doing so, they learn something most people never figure out:

Your shadow doesn't weaken you. Denying it does.

Once you face it, you stop being afraid of it. And once you stop being afraid of it, you can finally choose who you want to be, not out of fear, but out of truth.

That's the heart of code: it's not who you pretend to be. It's who you choose to be after seeing your whole self.

Shadow Work: The Rogue's Code

Face the shadow. Write the code. Move with both.

Choose one:

- List 3 values you *actually live by,* not the ones you talk about, but the ones your actions prove.
- What's one moment you betrayed your own code? What did it teach you?
- What part of yourself have you tried to hide that's actually a source of strength?
- Write one sentence that only you need to believe. The code that steadies you when no one else understands it.

Remember: your shadow holds power, not shame. When you own it, no one else can use it against you.

From Cutpurse to MasterMind

You started this journey as the Cutpurse, the one moving through side streets and shadowy corners, not because you had it all figured out, but because you refused to wait. You didn't ask for a map. You trusted your own motion.

You learned to move without permission. To observe without needing attention. To act without asking. To adapt without applause. To build without backup. To carry your own code, even when it didn't match the crowd's.

That's the Rogue's way.

Now, something is shifting.

You're no longer just surviving in the alleyways. You're starting to understand the systems. The patterns. The levers. You're not just slipping through cracks, you're seeing how the whole structure works.

The Rogue doesn't stay the Cutpurse forever.

At some point, instinct becomes strategy. Movement becomes precision. Observation becomes orchestration.

That's when the Rogue becomes the MasterMind.

What's coming next isn't louder, it's deeper. You've earned your way off the streets and into the game behind the game.

IV

The Operative

The Shadow conceals. The Operative engages.
Once you've chosen your role, you begin to use it. This part is
about precision moves, quiet influence, and building systems that
don't just respond to power, they redirect it. The Rogue stops
slipping past traps. They start resetting them. This isn't rebellion.
It's refinement.

The world plays its part.
The Rogue rewrites the scene.
This is where action becomes architecture.

Master the Escape Plan

"The Rogue doesn't run. They vanish when the time is right."
— The Whisper from the Shadows

Some exits feel like defeat. Others feel like freedom.

A Rogue knows the difference.

You don't need to stay loyal to a job, a title, a path, or a pattern just because you've invested time in it. Just because it once made sense doesn't mean it still does. Growth means reevaluation. And sometimes? Growth means leaving.

Most people are taught to associate leaving with failure. That walking away is a weakness, a surrender, a lack of endurance. The Rogue sees something different in the shadows of every exit: possibility.

The Rogue learns that escape isn't an act of desperation. It's a strategy. A shift. A clean cut between what was and what needs to be. Escaping, when done right, is not about cowardice, it's about clarity. It's not about being done. It's about being *ready*.

This isn't about quitting. This is about escaping. With clarity. With control. With intention.

Not Every Exit Is Failure

We're told to finish what we start. To be dependable. To stick things out. There's truth in that, sometimes, but the Rogue knows there's also a time to walk away.

Not every path is meant to be completed. Some roads lead to walls. Others circle endlessly. Wisdom isn't just knowing when to keep going. It's knowing when a direction no longer serves who you've become.

Leaving doesn't mean you've failed. It means you've learned.

There's a kind of strength that doesn't show up in standing your ground. It shows up in knowing when to let go. To release your grip on something you once loved. To stop pouring effort into a container with cracks you can't repair. That's not giving up. That's honoring your growth.

It's scary because leaving forces us to face uncertainty, but the alternative, staying in something that's slowly eroding who you are, is a slower form of loss.

I know that moment. I've lived it. I told myself I could hold out just a little longer. That if I just adjusted, softened, compromised, it would get better. That maybe I could be more patient. That maybe I was the problem.

I stayed quiet. Smiled through frustration. Folded myself smaller to keep the peace. And with each passing day, I stopped recognizing the version of me who was always compromising.

The truth? The longer I stayed, the smaller I became. My fire dimmed. My instincts dulled. I stopped speaking up, stopped trying new things, stopped reaching for the life I actually wanted, because I was too busy trying to make someone else's version of it work.

The MasterMind doesn't flinch at endings. They understand the exit is the move.

Every great Rogue has one more trick up their sleeve: knowing how to disappear when the time is right.

Why Staying Too Long Costs More Than Leaving

People think staying is safe. That if you just keep your head down and push forward, things will work out. Staying in the wrong job, relationship, or role too long doesn't just cost you time, it chips away at your clarity.

You start to shrink to fit it. You start to convince yourself it's not *that* bad. You mute parts of who you are to keep the peace, or the paycheck, or the illusion of stability.

Over time, that dulls your edge.

Syd Barrett didn't wait to be replaced. He left before he became a prisoner of something that no longer aligned. As a founding member of Pink Floyd, his early work shaped the soul of a generation, but when fame and pressure began to fracture his sense of self, he didn't fake his way through it. He stepped back. Disappeared. Not with a meltdown or a mic drop, but a retreat into a quieter life where he could just *be*.

He never returned to the spotlight. Never explained himself. He just left. And that's the power of a clean exit.

It's not about dramatics. It's about self-respect.

You don't need the world to understand why you walked. You only need to trust the part of you that knew it was time.

Let's flip this.

Imagine someone less famous. Someone maybe like you. A person who's been grinding at a job for six years. They started strong. Felt purpose. Felt pride. But somewhere along the way, that shifted. The passion thinned. The company culture soured. The ceiling dropped, but they stayed, because it paid the bills, because it was "good enough."

Now it's year six. They're tired and they've lost their spark. They're doing the job, but the job is doing them too.

One day, in a quiet moment, they realize: "I'm not stuck because of the job. I'm stuck because I haven't let myself imagine something different." So they start planning. Quietly. Updating a resume. Studying something new. Not broadcasting it, just building an escape, and when the moment's right, they slide out.

No drama. No bitterness. Just a clean break and a head held high.

That's a master move.

That's the exit that isn't about running away. It's about running *toward* something real.

The Exit Is a Move, Not a Reaction

People associate the word "escape" with desperation. With chaos. But the Rogue sees it differently.

A good escape is art.

It's prepped. It's considered. It's done with the same precision you've used to build your code, your focus, your quiet wins. You don't slam the door. You leave it unlocked because you know you'll never need to walk back through it again.

MasterMinds don't leave with flames. They leave with clarity, and usually? They leave long before anyone realizes they're gone.

Here's what a clean escape looks like:

- You've reflected - Not just on what's wrong, but on what you truly want.
- You've planned your next step - Not perfectly, but with enough structure to move.
- You've conserved your energy - Not to stay, but to leave strong.

A Rogue who walks instead of explodes keeps their power. Because they didn't hand it to anyone else. You don't owe anyone an explanation for why you need to leave something that no longer feeds your future.

But you *do* owe yourself the truth.

Leaving Isn't Just Physical

Not every escape is from a place. Sometimes, it's from a persona, a mask, or a story.

You might leave:

- A career you pursued because someone else said it was impressive
- A version of yourself you created to survive high school, or your first job, or a bad relationship
- An expectation that you've carried for years, quietly, heavily

MasterMinds don't just exit buildings. They exit roles. They exit patterns. They exit illusions. Sometimes, those are the hardest exits to make, because no one claps, no one throws a goodbye party.

You just feel lighter, and that's how you know you're finally free.

You Don't Have to Be Loud to Leave

Let the others shout.

The Rogue doesn't slam the door. They don't post a manifesto. They don't need the last word.

They just vanish. And when people finally realize they're gone, it's too late to stop them. Because the move already happened. The plan was already in place.

The exit wasn't improvised. It was earned.

Operative Directive: Write Your Escape Plan

The Rogue doesn't run from the fire. They walk out before the smoke ever rises.

Choose one:

- What space, role, or relationship have you stayed in too long? What's the first step toward stepping out?
- What identity or expectation are you ready to outgrow?
- Write a one-sentence exit strategy. Not to explain. Just to clarify.

Remember: Escape isn't the end. It's the beginning of precision.

The Clean Cut

Some people leave with fireworks. You won't be one of them. Because the
Rogue knows that real exits don't always come with noise. They don't require
a speech, a reckoning, or an audience. Sometimes they just require a decision.

There's a fantasy that we're sold. When someone wrongs you, you rise up.
You speak truth to power, slam your fist on the table, tell them off, take what
you're owed, and walk out like a movie ending. But real life rarely offers
such tidy closure.

Sometimes, the cleanest power move is the one where you say nothing at all.

The Myth of the Burnout Exit

The world romanticizes drama. Viral quit videos. Loud statements. The
emotional mic drop. It wants you to believe that if you don't make a scene,
your exit doesn't count. That if you don't burn the bridge, no one will know
how badly they treated you.

But you're not trying to be known for how you left. You're trying to live free after you leave.

Burnout exits are a reaction. A clean cut is a choice. And choice is where the Rogue moves best.

You don't need to perform rage. You don't need to explain your disappointment. You don't need to drag them into a final conversation where they pretend to care.

You just need to cut the tie and move.

Not with bitterness. With clarity.

The blade doesn't need to be big. It just needs to be sharp.

Signs You're Lingering Too Long

Sometimes you already know it's time to go, but you're waiting for something. An excuse. A push. A clean invitation to exit.

But the Rogue doesn't wait for the world to hand over closure.

Here's how you know you're already halfway out the door:

- You dread going in, not because it's hard, but because it's pointless.
- You rewrite your reasons for staying weekly.
- You're still doing the work, but your heart left six months ago.
- The mission is gone. Now you're just collecting checks, smiles, or status.
- You imagine leaving more often than you imagine improving it.

We think that staying longer means we're strong.

But sometimes, staying longer just means we've gotten good at tolerating what we shouldn't have to tolerate.

There is no bonus round for endurance. There is no gold star for staying in the wrong place until you collapse.

You are allowed to walk out when you know it's time. And you don't owe anyone a dramatic explanation.

When Clarity Replaces Closure

Closure is one of the most overrated ideas we've ever been sold. The belief that you must sit across from the person, the boss, the partner, the friend, and get a final moment. An understanding. Mutual respect. A bow wrapped around the pain.

But most people never give you that. Most situations don't earn it.

And that's okay. You don't need closure.

You need clarity.

You need to know the truth, not the version they'd try to sell you in a final meeting. You need to feel your own boundaries more than you need to hear their justification.

You need to trust your instinct when it says: "This isn't it. Not anymore."

Clarity is quiet. It doesn't clap for itself. It doesn't demand anything. It just settles in your bones like a steady certainty. And once you have that? The move becomes simple.

You don't plead. You don't provoke. You don't perform.

You just leave.

Story: Boundary, Not Burn

When I was seventeen, I worked in one of those tiny mall kiosks, you know the kind. Middle of the corridor, shiny lights, smiling too wide. I had already worked half a dozen odd jobs, but this one was different.

We were selling these reusable hand warmers, little pads that heated instantly when you snapped a metal disc inside. They were easy to demo, easy to pitch, and people loved them. I was good at it. I mean *really* good.

Sales were flying. I was outselling others on the floor, getting pulled aside by other vendors asking how I was doing it. And I was proud of myself. Because I was told I'd earn commission on top of my hourly. That every sale was more than just a smile. It was progress. A step toward something.

Then my check came.

Just hours. Nothing more. No commission. No bonus. No explanation.

I was furious. I had every reason to be. But I didn't yell. I didn't call HR. I didn't make a scene in the food court. I had another job lined up. I'd already planned to leave. This was just the final confirmation I needed.

So I walked.

No notice. No text. No call. Just silence.

It was the first time in my life I left a job like that. No flinch. No fight.

I remember walking through the mall that day and feeling something settle inside me, a sense of alignment. Like I'd finally learned how to exit without explaining myself to people who never intended to do right by me. That moment taught me something I'd carry forward into every chapter that followed:

You don't need to prove they were wrong.

You just need to prove to yourself that you're done.

The Blade You Carry

By the time you reach this phase of your Rogue path, you've sharpened your instincts. You know how to read a room. You know when your energy is being drained. And now? You know how to cut.

The clean cut isn't about rage. It's about respect for yourself, your time, your energy. It's a quiet statement that says: "I don't need to fight you. I just need to stop feeding you."

People might call it cold. Let them. Those who benefited from your silence will always resent your exit.

You're not cutting connection. You're cutting confusion.

You're not destroying bridges. You're deciding who gets to cross.

The Rogue doesn't burn things to feel powerful. They move so precisely, so intentionally, that the absence speaks louder than confrontation ever could.

Operative Directive: The Clean Cut

The Rogue doesn't run from the fire. They walk out before the smoke ever rises.

Choose one:

- What space, role, or relationship have you stayed in too long? What's the first step toward stepping out?
- What identity or expectation are you ready to outgrow?
- Write a one-sentence exit strategy. Not to explain. Just to clarify.

Remember: Escape is not an ending. It's a redirection of power.

Your clarity is the blade.

Use it.

The Quietest Weapon

> *"Loud power demands attention. Soft power makes them lean in."*
> — *The Whisper from the Shadows*

Most people think power needs to be loud. They think it looks like commands, spotlights, and statements. That it comes from speaking first, filling the air, or having the most followers in the room.

Rogues know better.

Rogues know there's a quieter kind of force. One that doesn't burn out, doesn't flinch, works in silence, and still shifts the outcome.

It's called soft power and when you learn how to use it, you stop chasing control.

You start carrying it.

The Mistake Everyone Makes

People confuse volume with influence.

The loudest voice in the room often masks the deepest insecurity. The Rogue isn't trying to win the room. They're reading it.

They assume the one talking the most has the most to say. They chase charisma like it's strategy. They mistake confidence for clarity, but presence isn't about filling space, it's about owning your energy.

The Rogue doesn't need to dominate the room. They just need the room to adjust slightly when they speak.

Soft power doesn't rush.
It doesn't force.
It doesn't fight for space.

It moves with such certainty that space opens on its own. The loudest voice might win attention. The quietest voice, when it lands just right, shifts the entire direction.

What Is Soft Power Really?

Soft power isn't weakness. It's awareness.

It's the ability to read the tempo of a room and speak when others have burned their words out. It's the kind of influence that doesn't need applause, because its results are undeniable.

Soft power looks like:

- Pausing before you speak, and letting the silence do half the work.
- Listening longer than others can stand.
- Making one question hit harder than ten declarations.
- Letting others exhaust themselves, then stepping in with clarity.

This isn't manipulation. It's mastery.

Rogues don't chase the spotlight, but they know exactly how to bend it when the time comes.

Soft Power vs. Status Games

There's a psychological difference between power and status.

Power is real. It's the ability to shape outcomes through presence, control, or action. Status is perception. It's how others rank you in the social pecking order.

Power moves in silence.
Status begs to be seen.

According to social psychologists like Dacher Keltner, people often confuse the two, but a Rogue never does. They know that status is borrowed, and power is earned. A person might have high status. Loud, liked, seen, but no real power to shift decisions. Another might speak rarely, be overlooked on paper, but carry the authority to shape direction with a single glance or question. That's soft power.

That's Rogue power.

It doesn't care who claps. It moves the room without needing to be the center of it.

Influence Isn't Performance

Not all leaders bark. Not all experts posture. Not all power wears a name tag.

Soft power is built over time, through observation, calibration, and presence. It's the person who doesn't say much, but when they *do* speak, it lands. People pause. The air shifts.

It's the way you enter a room without demanding anything and still get what you came for.

That doesn't happen by accident. It happens because you've watched, you've waited, you've chosen stillness instead of scrambling.

You don't perform influence.

You *become* it.

Story: You Didn't Get Credit. But You Controlled the Outcome

I know someone who moves like this every single day.

Her name is Shelly Fierro. Skell, to her friends. She's a visual designer, an artisan, and if you only looked at the final creative she delivers, you'd be impressed. However, you'd also be missing the real power.

What you wouldn't see is how often she's behind the scenes keeping projects on track, not because she's asked to, but because she's watching where things might fall. She's the one checking in when details slip, following up when timelines stretch, keeping communication flowing between teams who otherwise wouldn't speak.

She doesn't need credit.
She doesn't ask for recognition.
She doesn't grab the mic and announce how many fires she's put out.

The truth is, the projects succeed because of her, because of the structure and steadiness she builds quietly, consistently, deliberately.

Her power isn't loud, it's rooted, and reliable. Felt by everyone, even if they can't name it.

That's the Rogue way.

Real-World Rogue: John Krasinski

John Krasinski didn't try to outshine anyone. He didn't shout for attention or reinvent himself overnight. He just kept showing up. Curious, deliberate, watching the angles others missed.

First, we saw him as Jim Halpert, the quiet one with the sideways smirk in *The Office*. While other characters exploded with energy or chaos, he played it different. Understated. Observant. He said more with a glance than a monologue. No chase for main-stage charisma. No performance to steal scenes. Just subtle timing, quiet empathy, and one perfectly raised eyebrow.

Then something shifted.

He moved behind the camera, and he created. He built something new. He directed *A Quiet Place*, a film rooted in silence, tension, and presence. A story told more through stillness than speech.

Sound familiar?

That's Rogue energy.

He didn't announce a transformation. He just made one. Not by performing louder, but by choosing his moments, trusting his voice, and letting the work speak for itself.

That's soft power. And it lands harder than you think.

Building Your Quiet Force

Soft power isn't about volume. It's about *voltage.* The energy behind your presence.

You don't need to dominate a room to shape it. You just need to understand its rhythm. Here are some Rogue tactics that build soft power:

- **Speak last.** Let others show their cards first. Then respond with clarity.
- **Ask the question that changes the room.** Not more questions. *The* question.
- **Hold tension longer than others can.** Don't rush to fill the silence.
- **Observe before you act.** What people don't say is just as revealing as what they do.
- **Pick your moment.** You don't need to speak every time. Just the right time.

Presence isn't performance. It's power that chooses where to land.

When you master that kind of move? The room might not remember what you said, but they'll remember that *you* said it.

Operative Directive: The Soft Power Move

Influence isn't always seen, but it is always felt.

Choose one:

- This week, enter one meeting and don't speak for the first ten minutes. Watch what happens.
- Instead of adding your take, ask one strategic question. Let it guide the direction.
- Pick a conversation where you normally over-explain and just say less.

You don't have to shout to shift the outcome.

Soft power doesn't force the room.

It tilts it, just enough to change the outcome.

The Network Is the Knife

Not every weapon is sharp on its own. Some blades are forged in silence, shaped over time, passed hand to hand until they're exactly where they need to be.

That's how a Rogue sees connection.

This chapter isn't about popularity or performance. It's not about racking up followers or shaking every hand. It's about something quieter, sharper: Strategic alignment.

The Rogue doesn't network. They map. They don't collect people. They choose their crew with care, and when the moment comes?

They make one call.
One name.
One door.
One move that shifts everything.

The Myth of the Self-Made Rogue

Let's break the myth again. No one climbs alone.

The world loves to sell the self-made legend. The lone genius. The underdog who rose with nothing but grit and grind. But that story? It's missing key pages.

Even the most independent Rogue still had help. A whisper. A gatekeeper who looked the other way. A mentor who saw potential. A peer who vouched for them behind closed doors.

The difference? The Rogue doesn't brag about who they know.

They just move like the next door's already open.

The Map, Not the Mob

Other people chase popularity. The Rogue builds leverage.

Not everyone in your orbit is part of your operation. The ones who matter aren't always loud, but they hold keys. They know the back channels. The weak points. The hidden entries. That's why a Rogue doesn't broadcast their network. They read the board. They watch who opens doors. They pick the names that matter.

When the time comes, they don't need everyone. They need someone specific, and that name? That's the knife.

Questlove: The Connector in the Shadows

Ahmir "Questlove" Thompson is a drummer, producer, DJ, filmmaker, and cultural historian. You might know him as the bandleader of *The Roots*, the house band for *The Tonight Show Starring Jimmy Fallon*, but that's just the surface.

He's a bridge-builder. The kind of person who can text a dozen creative legends and get them in a room, not because he demands it, but because he's earned their respect. He moves behind the scenes, quietly shaping moments that define music, film, and culture.

He led The Roots into late night television without losing their soul. He directed *Summer of Soul*, a documentary that unearthed long-lost footage of the 1969 Harlem Cultural Festival, and let the story speak louder than his name. He curates brilliance, not for attention, but for impact.

His power isn't in being everywhere. It's in knowing who should be where.

That's a Rogue network in action. It doesn't shout. It moves like a whisper that reshapes the room.

Eiichiro Oda: The Cartographer of Trust

Oda is the mind behind *One Piece*, one of the most beloved and expansive stories in anime history. He doesn't chase interviews. He doesn't flood social media. He doesn't show up in your feed every day.

But his name? Carries weight.

Why? Because he's spent decades building a trusted network. Editors, animators, collaborators, that lets him shape a global phenomenon while staying almost entirely in the background.

When Netflix made the *One Piece* live-action series, Oda's involvement wasn't just a detail, it was the deal breaker. The project moved because he said yes, and when he said yes, it wasn't for exposure. It was because the right people had earned his trust.

His network is small, but it's sharp, and when he moves? The industry adjusts.

That's what a forged connection looks like.

Loud vs. Leveraged

There's a difference between being seen and being strategic.

The loud network is easy to spot.

It fills your feed.
Shouts every win.
Tags every name.
It's the kind of presence that floods the room, hoping someone notices and sometimes, it works for a while. Visibility doesn't equal value. Rogues don't build to be seen. They build to strike. A loud network claps the moment you move. A leveraged one moves the moment you need it.

The loud path says: "Get known by everyone."
The Rogue path says: "Be remembered by the right one."

It's the difference between a flare and a signal. One burns out fast, pulling attention in every direction. The other is quiet, directed, and lands exactly where it needs to. You don't need everyone watching. You need someone watching for the right reason.

Someone who knows you move clean.
Someone who knows when to make the call.

Someone who sees through the noise and says your name when it counts.

When the door is locked, the loud ones bang and rattle and ask to be let in.

The Rogue?

They already know who has the key and they don't knock. They slip through.

How to Sharpen the Knife

You don't need a crowd. You need a blade. Here's how you forge the kind of connections that cut clean:

- **Offer value without fanfare.** Be useful before you're visible.
- **Observe who opens doors.** Not who posts the most. Watch how influence actually moves.
- **Stay low, stay sharp.** You don't need to be in every room. Just remembered by the right people in one.
- **Let others win.** Sometimes, giving someone else the assist is what earns you the call later.
- **Make the ask when it matters.** Don't burn the knife swinging wildly. Use it when the door is locked tight.

Your network isn't just who you know. It's who knows you'll move clean when the time comes.

You Only Need One Blade

One of the biggest lies in the modern world is that you need to go viral to matter. That you need a platform, a podcast, a personal brand. That you need to know everyone.

You don't.

You need someone. Someone who sees you, who trusts you, who keeps your name in rooms you haven't stepped into yet.

When that name drops, and they call you in? You don't have to push.

You just have to step through.

Operative Directive: The Network Is the Knife

You don't need more followers. You need sharper allies.

Choose one:

- Identify one person in your orbit who quietly opens doors. Reach out. Thank them. See what they're building.
- Make one move this week that earns trust, not attention.
- Map your current network. Who's noisy? Who's quietly powerful? Who haven't you reached out to in too long?

Remember: You don't need an army. You just need the right name at the right time, and when that moment comes?

Move.

The Operative knew when to act. But the MasterMind knows when to disappear.

You've moved with precision.
Aligned with power.
Made exits clean and influence quieter than anyone expected.

Now it's time to stop playing the game everyone else sees, and start designing the one they don't.

V

The MasterMind

The Operative moves with skill. The MasterMind moves with intention.
At this level, there are no wasted steps. The Rogue has stopped surviving the game and started shaping it. This part is about long vision, subtle shifts, and mastering the art of not being noticed until it's too late to stop you. You don't need the spotlight. You move it.

The world reacts.
The Rogue orchestrates.
This is where strategy becomes a legacy.
Power shifts when others think nothing has changed.

The Game Behind the Game

**"The smartest Rogues don't play harder. They play better.
They change the board."**
— The Whisper from the Shadows

You're not reacting anymore. You're reading the room, setting the tempo, moving with purpose.

The Rogue who once moved out of necessity now moves with precision. You're done scrambling. Now you're thinking three moves ahead. Not to manipulate, but to maneuver. This isn't about deception. It's about direction.

You've mapped the system. You've tracked the patterns. You know when to speak, when to move, and when to disappear. You're no longer playing their game. You're reshaping the rules.

This is the MasterMind stage of the Rogue's path.

You're Not Just in the Game Anymore

Most people move through life playing the surface game. They follow the rules they're given. Chase what they're told to value. They work, respond, react. Rogues start that way too. But they don't stay there.

The MasterMind sees the system for what it is and more importantly, sees where it can be influenced. They notice patterns. Hidden openings. Human dynamics. And instead of forcing outcomes, they *guide* them.

They don't fight the game. They study it, understand it, and then start adjusting the levers everyone else is ignoring. This shift doesn't always feel dramatic. In fact, it's often subtle. Quiet. Then one day, you realize something: You're not responding to the world anymore. You're designing your role within it.

You're no longer asking, "How do I get ahead?" Instead, you're asking, "What system am I building and who does it serve?"

This is where you begin creating outcomes that align with your code. Influence rarely comes from the front of the room. It comes from the one who set the agenda before the meeting even began.

Think of it like this: the MasterMind doesn't just play the game. They quietly rewrite the rules while everyone else is still arguing over the last move.

This isn't about control. It's about leverage. The key isn't being loud, it's being deliberate.

Power in Silence, Strength in Planning

There's a moment every Rogue hits when they realize that not every truth needs to be spoken right away. Not every reaction deserves your energy. Sometimes, silence is the sharpest tool in your kit.

I learned that in a moment that cut deep.

A few years back, I was due for a performance review. I had been showing up early, staying late, solving problems no one else would touch. The results were there. The praise was there. Everyone, including my manager, acknowledged I was due for the next step.

This was supposed to be the meeting.
The moment.
The reward.

However, that's not how it went.

We went through the wins, the value, the growth. They nodded along like they agreed with all of it. Then, without hesitation, I was told there would be no raise. No title change. Just a "Good job," and a pivot to the next topic.

I felt the heat rise to my face. That tight sting behind the eyes. I wanted to say something sharp, to call it what it was.

A lie.
A stall.
A slap after years of quiet loyalty, but I didn't.

I paused. I let the silence hang heavy in the space between us. Then I thanked them, turned away, and walked out.

Not because I wasn't furious. I was, but because I realized something in that silence: Any words I spoke in anger would be used to define me, but silence. That was still mine to control.

I stayed. I kept delivering. Not for them, but for the leverage I knew I was building. I let my results stack up. No noise. Just quiet proof.

Eventually, I got the raise. Not out of pity. Not from pleading, but because I had made myself undeniable.

That's the move. That's the shift. Sometimes, silence doesn't mean defeat. Sometimes, silence sharpens the blade.

That's what the MasterMind understands.

People Are Systems Too

It's not just environments the MasterMind navigates. It's people as well, because at the heart of every system are the humans who run it, and people aren't logic puzzles.

They're stories.
Emotions.
Insecurities.
Patterns.

The Rogue who once moved alone now learns to read these stories, not to exploit, but to understand. The MasterMind doesn't dominate people. They *listen,* they observe, they move in alignment with what's needed, not just what they want.

Influence is earned. Not through noise, but through presence.

You've probably felt it before. That person who never has to raise their voice to command a room.

That's the kind of power you carry now.

Controlling the Tempo

MasterMinds don't just make smart moves. They make them at the *right time.*

Controlling tempo is one of the most overlooked skills in life, and yet, it changes everything.

Think of a great poker player. They don't just watch the cards, they watch the table. They read the room. They let others speak, overplay, or reveal more than they meant to.

Then they move.

There's actually science behind this. In communication research, it's often referred to as the **latency effect** or **strategic delay.** A pause before speaking that shifts how you're perceived. A 2018 study in the *Journal of Nonverbal Behavior* found that speakers who paused before answering were rated as more confident, thoughtful, and composed than those who responded immediately.

It's not hesitation. It's control. Pauses give weight to your words. They create space. And that space signals presence.

In leadership studies, measured speech patterns, especially deliberate silence, are consistently associated with perceived authority and clarity. Negotiators know this too. A Harvard Law School report found that most concessions occur *after* a pause, because silence disrupts automatic responses, often pushing rushed speakers to reveal more than they intend.

The MasterMind doesn't fill the silence. They let it stretch, because the longer you can sit with tension, the more power you hold over what comes next.

The MasterMind learns this same rhythm:

- In meetings, they let silence build just long enough to surface real insight.
- In conflict, they speak only when their words will shift the room, not just fill the air.

- In strategy, they wait. Observe. And act when the result will land clean.

It's not about slowing down. It's about knowing *when* speed matters.

Waiting isn't weakness. It's timing. And the one who controls the tempo often controls the outcome.

Final Moves: Begin the Game Behind the Game

The Rogue who knows the system can bend it. The one who built it? Controls it.

Choose one:

- Where in your life are you still playing the surface game, reacting instead of shaping?
- What system (job, relationship, routine) do you now see more clearly? What's one deliberate move you can make this week that pulls a thread?
- What's one thing you've been rushing that actually requires patience?

Remember: You don't need to win louder. You just need to win *smarter*. You're not reacting anymore. You're orchestrating.

The Rogue is Never Lost

There's a moment that every Rogue reaches. A realization. A pause. A breath. Not because they're stuck, but because they've finally stopped running.

Not from something. Not toward something. But with full awareness of where they are.

That's when it clicks. You're not lost. You're just off the main road. That's exactly where you were always meant to be.

The maps you were handed growing up, the ones drawn by systems, expectations, institutions, were never designed with you in mind. They had neat labels, safe routes, clearly marked exits. They didn't account for your instincts. Your timing. Your code.

So you learned to read the world differently. You stopped following the signs and started tracking something deeper. You started trusting your own route. There were moments it felt like wandering. Detours, delays, dark corners where the light didn't reach. There were missteps and false starts. Days when you doubted the path, and even yourself.

Every step taught you something.

You learned how to move without permission. How to see without being seen. How to act without waiting for applause. How to leave without explanation.

How to trust your timing. How to design your own mission on purpose.

You didn't just follow the map. You became it. Now you don't need a path, because you are the path.

When someone asks how you got here, you'll shrug and smile. You won't be able to point to one clear road. You'll point to the edges, the alleys, the high rooftops and low tunnels. The pauses. The pivots. The people you picked up along the way or left behind.

That's the truth of the Rogue. We're not linear, we're not official, we're not easy to track, but we always know where we're going. Even if no one else can see the way we do. That's what makes us effective. That's the edge we carry.

You've made it. From Cutpurse to Lookout. From Shadow to MasterMind. You didn't just learn the Rogue's tools. You *became* one.

You've mastered the art of moving differently. Now? You'll move through life with a precision others won't always understand. That's okay.

You didn't become a Rogue to be understood. You became a Rogue to be *free*.

This book wasn't about teaching you how to be sneaky. It wasn't about tricks or manipulation.

It was about waking up your awareness.

It was about reminding you of the power that comes from moving with clarity in a noisy world. From trusting your instincts when the crowd zigs and you know it's time to zag. From knowing that just because no one else can see the opportunity, doesn't mean it isn't there.

Rogues don't wait to be invited. They make their own entry points.

That's what you've done here.

You answered the call. You stepped onto the street alone. You learned how to watch, how to wait, how to move. You explored your shadow, not to destroy it, but to understand it. You sharpened your code. You chose your exits. You stopped seeking approval.

Now? You're moving like a MasterMind.

Not because everything is figured out. Because you finally know how to figure it out. That's the real power of the Rogue: not certainty, but adaptability. You can walk into unfamiliar terrain and trust your footing. You can be underestimated and smile because you've planned ten steps ahead. You don't need to be the loudest in the room. You just need to be the one who knows when to act.

You've built this version of yourself the Rogue way.

Step by step.
In silence.
With clarity.
Through experience.

So take a breath and really feel it.

You didn't need to follow anyone's blueprint. You didn't need permission. You didn't need perfection. You just needed your instincts, your timing, your willingness to move even when the way wasn't clear.

Now you're here. Not at the end of the story, but at the beginning of a new one.

Being a Rogue isn't about reaching a destination. It's about having the tools to *keep choosing,* again and again, what's right for you. To shift when others stall. To slip out when others stay stuck. To say no when others say yes just to fit in. To walk alone without fear and to know how to spot your people when they appear.

You've learned to listen to silence.
To read the room.
To move in the dark.

You are the Rogue, and you are never lost.

Not because you always know the route, but because you've learned to trust yourself even when the map doesn't exist. That's your legacy now. That's your advantage.

This is where the book ends, but the work continues.

You'll keep refining your code. You'll keep designing clean exits and wise entrances. You'll keep listening to your instincts. You'll keep building the kind of life that doesn't require applause to be meaningful.

A Rogue doesn't move for the crowd. They move for the mission. And yours? Only you can define it.

So go on. Vanish if you need to. Reappear when you're ready. Shape the game without playing it.

Remember, The Rogue is Never Lost. They just know where to walk when no one else is looking.

> **"If you've made it this far, then you already know. The Rogue never needed a map, they just needed a reason."** — The Whisper

from the Shadows

The Next Class Begins

> **"A true Rogue doesn't block the alley. They leave signs only the ready will see."**
> — The Whisper from the Shadows

You don't always know when you're being watched. Someone out there is watching you move. They see the way you make space for silence. The way you hold the line without drawing a weapon. The way you vanish when the noise gets too loud, but always seem to return sharper than before.

They don't know what it means yet, but it resonates.

You've walked this road without applause. You've learned to slip out the side door when the room didn't fit. You've survived what others never noticed. You've made decisions that no one will ever see, and still, you made them well.

Now someone else is standing in the doorway. They don't have the code yet. They don't know what a clean exit feels like. They've never held their silence long enough to learn who to trust. But they're ready. And you are proof that the path can be walked.

You didn't ask to be a guide. Most Rogues don't. The moment you moved with intention instead of fear, you lit a kind of signal. Not a flare. Not a beacon. A glint. A reflection. The flash of a blade tucked just out of sight.

The kind of light that only another Rogue would recognize.

They've found this book because they're looking for another way. They may not know what that means yet. But they know what it doesn't mean: obey, perform, beg, repeat. They're ready to slip past the noise and find something real.

You? You're already holding the door.

You didn't just read these pages. You *lived* them. You built your exits and your boundaries. You chose silence over spectacle. You made your own map.

You trusted the long game. You sharpened your edges. You moved on instinct, and over time, that instinct became clarity. And now, someone else is looking for permission to trust theirs.

You don't need to teach them. You don't need to warn them. Just don't disappear completely.

Let them see what survival with soul looks like. Let them see that you can live like this, strategic, clear, powerful, without turning cold. Let them see that you can hold your own without losing your heart.

The next path isn't stealth. It isn't speed. It's vow. It's fire. It's the Rogue's unlikely twin: The Paladin.

Where Rogues learn to disappear, Paladins learn to *stand*. Where Rogues master silence, paladins master truth. Sometimes, the Rogue becomes the very thing they never expected to be: Visible. Accountable. Devoted to something beyond themselves.

It doesn't mean losing what you've built. It means *choosing* when to step forward. It means becoming the kind of presence you once hid from.

You'll do it differently. You'll do it with layers. With caution. With depth. Only a Rogue knows how to guard something without putting it in chains. Only a Rogue knows how to fight with clarity instead of noise.

So leave the alley door cracked. Leave a mark where only a few will know to look. Leave the final lock half-turned.

Not for legacy. Not for credit. Just in case someone else needs a way in. You made it this far without a spotlight. Now it's time to carry a torch.

Quietly. Powerfully. Rogue-born. Paladin-ready.

> *"The Rogue who helped you may never know your face. But the one you help will never forget your silence."* — *Scrap of black cloth, stitched with threadbare gold.*

Thank you for reading.
Thank you for moving.
Thank you for surviving.

The next class is arriving, and this time, you're already watching from the shadows.

Welcome, MasterMind.

The Paladin waits.

The Rogue's Pocket Guide

You don't need to play D&D to speak Rogue. These terms are metaphors for moving smarter, quieter, and sharper in the real world.

CORE CONCEPTS

Rogue — A strategist, not a thief. Thrives on awareness, adaptability, and quiet power. Doesn't win with noise, wins with timing.

The Cutpurse — The scrappy starter phase. You move before you're "ready." Mistakes are your mentors. Survival is your teacher.

The Lookout — The observer phase. You study patterns, read rooms, and anticipate moves before they happen. Awareness is your first weapon and sometimes your only one.

The Shadow — Where you hone instincts and boundaries. Not hiding, observing. You learn who you are when no one's watching.

The MasterMind — The Rogue's apex. You don't react; you design the game. Others play checkers. You're already flipping the board.

TOOLS & TACTICS

Blade — Your focus. Precision over force. (Example: One sharp sentence that ends a debate.) The edge you sharpen is often your presence.

Lock — Any barrier. Rogues study the mechanism, then pick it or leave it. A lock isn't a challenge; it's a question.

Clean Exit — A vanish without drama or debt. Traces fade; bridges stay intact. You leave, and the silence says more than a speech ever could.

Escape Plan — A prepped exit (financial, emotional, social). Rogues plan before they're cornered. A pivot, not a panic.

Silent Step — A pivot without announcement. Changing jobs, habits, or paths, no spotlight, no speech. Just movement.

Disguise — A temporary posture. Not deception, adaptation. Rogues change their surface to access different rooms, but their core stays intact.

Signal — A quiet sign sent to the right people. Not a post. Not a pitch. Just a moment that says: *"I see you."*

MINDSET & MOVES

Code — Your unwritten rules. Not for applause, for alignment. (Example: "Never beg for a seat at a table I built.") Your code is what keeps you sharp when the noise starts to blur your vision.

Dodge — Sidestepping fools' battles. Not fear, discretion. Not silence, strategy.

Tempo — Controlling the pace. Rogues let others exhaust themselves first, then act when the field is clear.

Street Skill — A small, sharp habit to train instinct. (Example: Pausing 5 seconds before replying.) It's less about performance, more about pattern recognition.

The Play — Your long game. Rogues think in layers, not steps. The win is rarely immediate, but it's always intentional.

Lag — The intentional delay. Pausing your move to gather insight, create tension, or let others misstep first. Rogues don't rush. They time.

Mirror — The ability to reflect what others expect, without becoming it. Used to disarm, blend in, or learn. A mirror doesn't absorb, only shows what's there.

NAVIGATING SYSTEMS

The Board — The system you're in (work, society, family). Rogues map it, then move differently. You don't fight the game; you learn it better than they do.

The Game — Social or professional dynamics. Rogues rewrite the rules, quietly. Influence over visibility.

Hidden Door — The overlooked gap. (Example: The quiet ally who opens more doors than the loud boss.) Some opportunities don't knock. You find them behind the bookshelf.

Mask — A role you wear to navigate unsafe spaces. Useful, sometimes necessary, but toxic if forgotten.

Safehouse — Your recharge space (place, ritual, person). Where you shed armor and remember who you are when no one's asking you to perform.

Thread — A barely visible path forward. Thin, fragile, and easy to miss. Real Rogues don't always see the full staircase. They pull the thread until it reveals the way.

The Fog — The noise. The overwhelm. The chaos meant to keep you spinning. Rogues learn to pause, let it settle, and move only when the path is visible again.

> *"A thief steals gold. A Rogue steals opportunity. This is your lexicon of leverage."*

Acknowledgments

This book was built like a back-alley map, one decision, one boundary, one hard-earned truth at a time. Every word was chosen with intention. Every page is a reflection of the path I've walked: quiet, uncertain, often unseen, but always mine.

To my wife - Thank you for being my constant signal fire. The warmth I return to. You've always seen the version of me hiding just beneath the surface, and you've never asked me to be anyone else. That's the kind of love that changes everything.

To my daughter - You are the quiet strength I hope to pass on. The reason I learned to move differently. May the world you grow into hold space for softness and edge, for wonder, wildness, Rogues, and dreamers alike.

To my brother and sister - Jimmy and Star - your presence has always been part of my map. You've been with me since the beginning, and in every version of this journey, there's a place carved out that has your name on it.

To my mom - Thank you for the encouragement, for the freedom to explore, and for giving me the space to find my own way. I still feel your belief in the quiet moments when I need it most.

To my circle - Alexa, Shelly, Zac, Logan, and Michael - Your fingerprints are all over these pages. Through your support, your honesty, and your patience, you helped me find clarity in the fog. Thank you for being real.

To you, the reader - Thank you for slipping in. For walking this path beside me. For trusting your own instincts, even when the world asked you to ignore them.

This book is for the one who moves differently. Who lives in the margins. Who questions, adapts, resists, survives. For the one who knows that clarity isn't loud and neither is power.

If this book found you at the right time, it means you were already on your way.

You didn't need this book to become a Rogue.

You just needed someone to remind you that you already are.

May your shadow stay sharp.

May your code stay clear.

And may your next move be yours alone.

About the Author

Todd Campbell is a writer, analyst, and architect of quiet magic.

He believes that wonder is a skill, that intention shapes reality, and that even the smallest rituals can bring us back to who we really are. His work is part grimoire, part map, written not just in theory, but in motion.

Todd lives between the world that is and the one he's still building. A place where Wizards return to themselves, Rogues rewrite the rules, and everyone is invited to walk their own path with power, presence, and permission.

He still writes most of his spells by hand, and he rarely takes the same road twice.

You can connect with me on:

https://www.toddtheauthor.com

https://linktr.ee/Todd_The_Author

Also by Todd Campbell

Todd Campbell writes books for everyday adventurers, blending self-mastery, fantasy archetypes, and real-world transformation.

His *Everyday Adventurer* series invites readers to grow through metaphor, choice, and reflection. Drawing wisdom from classic RPG classes like the Wizard, Rogue, and beyond. These books are for anyone learning to move through life with quiet power, sharper instincts, and a story worth reshaping.

Think Like a Wizard
"Wizards aren't born. They're written. One page at a time." The Unknown Archmage

Think Like a Wizard is a motivational guide for anyone who's ever felt stuck, average, or lost in the grind. Inspired by fantasy role-playing games, this book blends real-world stories, actionable insights, and spellbook-style rituals to help awaken your potential.

You don't need glowing eyes or a tower in the clouds, just a curious mind and the courage to keep learning.